U0019913

跟李伯伯學英文

Learning English from Uncle Lee：Page 21

Page 21

中英對照

李家同 ◆ 著

康士林
鮑端磊 ◆ 譯

官月淑 ◆ 繪

國人增進英文程度、
國外學習中文者都將受益 （自序）

　　《第二十一頁》，聽說很受讀者的歡迎，九歌因此而推出中翻英的版本，對我來說，是一件很光榮的事，尤其讓我很不好意思的是，九歌請了輔大英語系康士林和鮑端磊兩位教授來翻譯，他們英文好，中文也好。我的文章，經過他們譯成英文以後，更加有趣了。

　　我們在台灣的人，可以利用這本書來學英文，因為我們平時沒有能力讀英文的小說，如果我們要小孩子唸狄更司的小說，一定會發現裡面太多的生字，而讀這一本書，應該是容易得多了。

　　要讀這本書，你不妨先從中文開始，將一段中文文章試著譯成英文，你當然一定譯得不好，但好歹都是練習，然後再和這本書的英文翻譯比較一下，相信更可以欣賞這兩位教授的功力。

　　至於海外的中國人，以及在英美想學中文的人，這本書可以幫助你學中文。你可以先讀中文，如果你看懂了，那就很好。如果看不懂，就可以看看英文的部份。

　　你也可以試著將中文翻譯成英文。

　　我也非常感激這本書有如此好的插畫，我覺得也許有些人會因為有這些插畫而買這本書。

　　國人有需要增進英文程度，國外正有讀中文的熱潮，這本書對兩者都有用。感謝九歌，感謝兩位教授，我們都將受益。

李家同　二〇〇七年九月

目　錄

下輯　李伯伯的英語課

李伯伯說故事

第二十一頁
Page 21

鮑端磊　譯

　　楊漢威再看了第二十一頁，想起他最後的一課就停在第二十一頁，十幾年來，張教授顯然一直記掛他⋯⋯

　　念完了習題，他說：「張老師，我已經會了，請您放心。」

　　Yang Han-wei looked again at page 21. He remembered his very last class was on page 21. Even after more than ten years, Professor Chang was apparently still worried about him... He read through the exercises, and then said, "Professor Chang, I can do it now. Please don't worry about me any longer."

張教授是我的老師，也是我們大家都十分尊敬的老師，他在微生物學上的成就，可以說是數一數二的，他的專書，也被大家列為經典之著。張教授終身投入教育，桃李滿天下，我們這些和微生物有關的人，多多少少都應該算是張教授的學生。

張教授身體一直很健朗，可是畢竟歲月不饒人，張教授近年來健康狀況大不如前。去年曾經有過一次住院的紀錄。今年，他再度住院，可是他的情形每況愈下。張教授是個頭腦清楚的人，當然知道他的大限已到。他是一個非常開朗的人，也有宗教信仰，所以他對死亡很

respect（v.）尊敬
expertise（n.）專門知識、專門技術
microbiology（n.）微生物學
monograph（n.）專書

regard（v.）把……看作，把……認為
education（n.）教育、培養、訓練
possibly（adv.）也許，可能

PROFESSOR CHANG was my teacher. He was the teacher we all respected the most. His expertise was microbiology, and if he wasn't the very best at it, he was close enough to be second best. His monographs were regarded by many as a Bible. Professor Chang put his all into education. He had more students than anyone could possibly count. We and everyone involved with him for the study of microbiology were in one way or the other students of Professor Chang.

Professor Chang's health had always been superb, but of course ultimately it became less than ideal. In recent years, his health simply was not what it once had been. A year earlier, he had to check into the hospital once. This particular year, he was again hospitalized. His condition was gradually getting worse and worse. Now, Professor Chang was very perspicacious, and he of

---

count（v.）計算、總計
involved（adj.）與……有關的
superb（adj.）極好的
ultimately（adv.）最後、終極地

particular（adj.）特定的
hospitalize（v.）使住院治療
perspicacious（adj.）有洞察力的

能接受，他說他也沒有什麼財產要處理，但是他十分想

念他的學生，有些學生一直和他有聯絡，也都到醫院來

看過他，但有好多學生已經很久沒有和他聯繫了。

　　張教授給了我一份名單，全是和他失聯的學生，要

我將他們一一去找出來，一般說來，找尋並不困難，大

多數都找到了。有幾位在國外，也陸陸續續地聯絡上

了，有些特地坐了飛機回來探病，有些打了長途電話

來。在這一份名單中，只有一位學生，叫做楊漢威，我

---

estate（n.）財產、資產　　　　track（n.）追蹤、聯絡
interaction（n.）互動

course knew very well that his end was drawing near. Always a very happy man, he also had his religious faith to rely on, and so he could accept death. He said that although he had no estate that needed plans and attention, he really missed his students.

Some of his students had always stayed in touch with Professor Chang. They came to visit him in the hospital. There were many other students, however, with whom he had no interaction for a very long time.

Professor Chang gave me a list of names, and every name on that list was of a student he had lost track of. He wanted me to find them, one by one. On the whole, finding them was not really very difficult. I found almost all of them. Some were abroad, but little by little they "reported in," you might say. A few even booked flight tickets and flew back to visit him in the hospital. Some made long distance telephone calls to

---

abroad（adv.）在國外、到國外　　　report（v.）報告、報導

們誰都不認得他，所以我也一直找不到他。後來，我忽然想起來，張教授一直在一所兒童中心教小孩子英文和數學，也許楊漢威是那裡的學生。果真對了，那所兒童中心說楊漢威的確是張教授的學生，可是他國中時就離開了，他們也幫我去找他，可是沒有找到。

就在我們費力找尋楊漢威的時候，張教授常常在無意中會說：「第二十一頁」。晚上說夢話，也都是：「第二十一頁」。我們同學們於是開始翻閱所有楊教授寫過的書，都看不出第二十一頁有什麼意義，因為張教授

mathematics（n.）數學、數學運算、數學應用

talk with him. But on that list there was one student by the name of Yang Han-wei, and none of us knew who he was. So it happened that I just could not find the fellow. Then, after a while, it came to me out of the blue one day that Professor Chang had always taught on the side at a social center for children. He taught mathematics and English. Perhaps this Yang Han-wei was one of his students there. It turned out to be exactly that way. The social center confirmed that Yang Han-wei had indeed been Professor Chang's student, but had left the center and its classes during his high school years. The people at the center said they'd help find him for me, but they didn't succeed.

During the very days we were going through all this trouble searching for this Yang fellow, Professor Chang would half unconsciously murmur the words "Page 21." At night, while he was dreaming, we would hear "Page 21." My classmates and I began to leaf through all the books Professor Chang had written, but

---

confirm（v.）確認、證實　　　　unconsciously（adv.）無意識地

此時身體已經十分虛弱，我們不願去問他第二十一頁是
怎麼一回事。

張教授找人的事被一位記者知道了，他將張教授找
楊漢威的故事在媒體上登了出來，有很多電台和電視台
都做了同樣的尋人啟事。這個記者的努力沒有白費，楊
漢威現身了。

我那一天正好去看張教授，當時醫院已經發出了張
教授的病危通知，本來張教授可以進入加護病房，但他
堅決不肯，他曾一再強調他不要浪費人類寶貴的資源，
我去看他的時候，他的聲音已經相當微弱了。

---

frail（adj.）身體虛弱的 juncture（n.）重要關頭
reporter（n.）報告人、記者 critical（adj.）關鍵性的、危急的
splash（n.）轟動

we could not discover the meaning of "Page 21." His health was getting frailer by the day, and we did not want to bother him by asking what this Page 21 business meant.

It so happened that a news reporter came to know of Professor Chang's trying to find his students, and he put the story out in the media. The news made quite a splash, and radio and television stations jumped all over it. "The Search" became a hot story. The efforts of the journalist did not go wasted. Yang Han-wei appeared.

On that same day, I went to visit Professor Chang. At that juncture, the hospital had already upgraded his condition to "critical." Although he qualified for a bed in the intensive care unit, he insisted he did not want it. Over and over again he emphasized he had no desire to waste medical resources. When I saw him that day, his

---

qualify（v.）合格、有資格　　　　insist（v.）堅持、堅決
intensive（adj.）密集的　　　　　emphasize（v.）強調、著重

　　楊漢威是個年輕人，看上去只有二十幾歲，完全是勞動階級的模樣，他匆匆忙忙地進入病房，自我介紹以後，我們立刻告訴張教授楊漢威到了。張教授一聽到這個好消息，馬上張開了眼睛，露出微笑，也用手勢叫楊漢威靠近他。張教授的聲音誰都聽不見，楊漢威將耳朵靠近他的嘴，居然可以聽到張教授，他用極大的聲音靠近張教授的耳朵，從張教授的表情來看，他一定是聽見楊漢威的話了。

　　我們雖然聽不見張教授的話，但聽得見楊漢威的話，聽起來是張教授在問楊漢威一些問題，楊漢威一一回答。我記得楊漢威告訴張教授，他沒有念過高中，但

---

appearance（n.）外貌、外表　　　immediately（adv.）立即、馬上

voice was quite weak.

Yang Han-wei was a young person. He seemed to be in his twenties. Everything in his appearance said he belonged to the working class. He rushed into the hospital room, and after telling us who he was, we immediately delivered the message to Professor Chang. His student Yang Han-wei had just arrived.

When Professor Chang heard the good news, he right away opened his eyes. A smile spread across his face, and he waved Yang over to his side.

Professor Chang's voice was now so soft that no one could hear it, and this Yang fellow practically put his ear against the man's mouth. Incredibly, he could hear what Professor Chang was saying. Yang spoke

---

spread（v.）展開

念過了補校，他一再強調他從來沒有學壞，沒有在

KTV做過事，也沒有在夜市裡賣過非法光碟，他現在

是個木匠，平時收入還可以。生活沒有問題，還沒有結

婚。

張教授聽了這些回答以後，顯得很滿意，他忽然叫

楊漢威到他的枕頭後面去拿一本書，這本書是打開的。

張教授叫楊漢威開始念打開的那一頁。這本書顯然是一

---

certain（adj.）某些
stress（v.）強調、著重

astray（adv.）離開正道、誤入歧
途

loudly, and directly into his ear, and we could tell from the expression on his face that Professor Chang surely heard his words. Although we could not hear Professor Chang, we knew what Yang was saying. It sounded as if Professor Chang asked him certain questions, and Yang answered them one after the other. I recall he told Professor Chang he had not gone to senior high school, but took special classes to supplement his education. He kept stressing he had never been led astray by bad company, that his line of work had nothing to do with the KTV industry, and he didn't have a business selling pirated CDs in night markets. He was a carpenter now, and made a decent wage. His life was free of problems, and he hadn't yet married.

Professor Chang appeared to be satisfied with the answers. He suddenly asked Yang Han-wei to step in back of his pillow and pick up a book that was placed there. The book was already open. Professor Chang told

---

carpenter（n.）木匠　　　　　還不錯的
decent（adj.）體面的、像樣的、　wage（n.）工資

本英文入門的書，這一頁是有關verb to be的過去式，有I was，You were等等的例子。楊漢威大聲地念完以後，張教授叫他做接下來的習題，楊漢威開始的時候，會犯錯，比方說，他常將were和was弄混了，每次犯了錯，張教授就搖搖頭，楊漢威會偷偷地看我，我也會打pass給他，越到後來，他越沒有錯了。習題做完了，楊漢威再靠近去，然後楊漢威告訴我們，張教授說：「下課了，你們可以回去了。」。張教授露出了一種安詳的微笑，他又暗示他有話要說，楊漢威湊了過去，這次，楊漢威忽然說不出話來了。過了幾秒鐘以後，他告訴我們，張教授說：「再見」。

---

elementary（adj.）基本的、初級的　　色、不同的
various（adj.）各種各樣、形形色　　err（v.）犯錯誤、出差錯

him to begin reading where the page was all ready for him. It seemed the book was an English textbook, a very elementary introduction to the language. That particular page dealt with the past verb tense of the verb "to be." It had various examples like "I was," "you were," and so on.

Yang Han-wei read it all in a loud voice, and then Professor Chang told him to go on to the next exercises. In the beginning, Yang made a few mistakes. For example, he mixed up "were" with "was." Every time he erred, Professor Chang shook his head, and Yang would throw me a secret glance. I'd lob him a pass, and by the time he got to the end, he wasn't making mistakes any longer. The exercises finished, Yang Han-wei leaned closer to him again. Yang told us what Professor Chang was saying. "Class is over now. You can go." Professor Chang relaxed into a peaceful smile. He indicated he had something he wanted to say. Yang Han-wei hurried

---

glance（n.）一瞥、看一眼　　　　indicate（v.）指出、表明

張教授就這樣離開了我們，楊漢威沒有將書蓋上，他翻回他開始念的那一頁，這是第二十一頁。他告訴我張教授在他國中時，仍叫他每週日去他的研究室，替他補習英文和數學，可是他家實在太窮了，經常三餐不繼，他實在無心升學，當時他玩心又重，就索性不去了。小孩子是不敢寫信的，他知道張教授一直在找他，卻一直沒有回去，但他一直記得張教授的叮嚀，就是不可以變壞，不可以到夜市去賣盜版光碟，不可以去KTV打工，不可以去跳八家將。他也記得張教授一再地強調他應該有一技隨身，所以他就去做一位木匠師傅

---

flip（v.）翻閱、瀏覽　　　　　tutor（v.）輔導、指導

over. This time, however, Yang suddenly could not find the words to speak. Seconds later, he told us that Professor Chang said "Goodbye."

So, that was the way Professor Chang left us. Yang Han-wei had not even closed the book. He had flipped the pages back to page 21. He said at his middle school, Professor Chang had him report to his office every Sunday, where he gave him special tutoring in English and mathematics. His family was so poor that scraping three meals together every day was already hard enough. He simply had no heart for studies. All he wanted to do was enjoy himself. So he soon stopped visiting Professor Chang's office.

Children do not dare to write letters. He was aware Professor Chang kept searching for him, but he never came back. All the while, however, he remembered Professor Chang's strongest directives. Put simply, by all

---

scrape（v.）勉強餬口　　　　　　　directive（n.）指令、指示、教誨

的學徒，現在手藝已經不錯了。等到他生活安定下來以

後，他又去念了補校，所以他對verb to be的過去式，

有點概念，但是不太熟。

　　　　楊漢威再看了第二十一頁，想起他最後的一課就停

在第二十一頁，十幾年來，張教授顯然一直記掛他，也

想將這一課教完。

---

pirate（v.）非法翻印、盜版　　　rite（n.）儀式、慣例
performance（n.）表演　　　　　impersonate（v.）扮演、模仿

means, he was not to "become bad." He was not to sell pirated CDs in some night market, or get a job in a KTV parlor. He was not to join performances of "bajiajiang," an evil-cleansing rite in which eight men impersonating eight ghost figures dance and lead a procession for religious festivals in Taiwan. He also clearly remembered Professor Chang's emphasis on finding a way to make a decent living. That is why he found a master carpenter and became his apprentice, and why he worked well now as a skilled laborer. After his life had become more stable, he attended an evening school. He had a general idea of the past tense for the English "to be," but now he couldn't remember it all.

Yang Han-wei looked again at page 21. He recalled his last class had ended on page 21. After more than ten years, Professor Chang was apparently still worried about him and wanted to finish that lesson once and for all.

---

apprentice（n.）學徒、徒弟　　　　stable（adj.）穩定的、可靠的

　　張教授的告別式簡單而隆重，教堂裡一張桌子上放了張教授的遺像，旁邊放了那本英文課本，而且打開在第二十一頁上，桌上的一盞檯燈照著這一頁，因為這是宗教儀式，只有神父簡單的講道，也沒有人來長篇大論地說張教授有多偉大。但是神父請楊漢威上台來，楊漢威將最後一課的習題朗誦了一遍，他有備而來，當然都沒有錯。念完了習題，他說：「張老師，我已會了，請您放心。」然後他走到桌子前面，闔上了書，將檯燈熄滅，這一堂課結束了。

---

farewell（n.）送別會、告別式
solemn（adj.）莊嚴的、隆重的
portrait（n.）肖像、畫像

priest（n.）牧師、神父、神職人員
preach（v.）佈道、講道
sermon（n.）佈道、說教

Our farewell service for Professor Chang was both solemn and simple. There was a table at the church with his portrait upon it. By its side was a copy of the English textbook, opened to page 21. A light sent its rays upon that page. Since it was a religious service, a Catholic priest preached a simple sermon. No one stepped forward to talk on and on of how terrific a man Professor Chang was, what a giant, and all of that. Instead, the priest asked Yang Han-wei to stand at the lectern and go through his last lesson. Of course he came well prepared, and handled the English flawlessly. When he finished the exercise, he said, "Professor Chang, I can do it now. Please don't worry about me anymore."

Then he walked to the front of the table, closed the cover of the book, and extinguished the light. Our last class thus ended.

---

terrific（adj.）非常好的、了不起的　　extinguish（v.）熄滅
lectern（n.）讀經台、講台　　thus（adv.）以此方式、因此
flawlessly（adv.）完美無暇地

我們這些學生都上了張教授的最後一堂課，他這次沒有提到微生物，他只教了我們一個道理：「你們應該關心不幸的孩子」。這也是我一生中最重要的一堂課。

——原載二○○六年一月五日《聯合報・副刊》

entire（adj.）全部的、整個的

So, that is how a group of us students went to class with Professor Chang for the last time. This time he didn't say a single word about microbiology. To put it in his own words, his lesson for us was "Show a little care for unfortunate youth." That was the most important class I attended in my entire life.

我的故事
My Story

鮑端磊　譯

　　如果我們成天想到自己如何厲害，會越來越驕傲，越來越沒有同情心。如果我們成天假想自己非常不幸，我們就會變得謙卑而又有同情心。

　　If all day long we think about how great we are, we become more and more proud of ourselves, and find less and less compassion in our hearts.

　　If all day long we imagine how miserable we are, we will become humble, and develop hearts full of compassion.

每一個人都有功課非常好的同學，我的同學老張就是我同學中功課超級好的一位。但是老張和很多資優學生不一樣，他一直非常願意幫助我們這些功課不好的同學。我們初一開始就是同班同學，那個時候，幾何常常令我沮喪，我老是弄不清楚如何加補助線。平時我們不管，一到考試近了，我們就慌了起來，好在老張永遠肯做義務家教，週六下午，我們幾乎全體留在教室裡，聽老張教我們如何解題，他也會教我們英文，我一直不懂現在完成式和過去式的分別，全班就只有老張懂，他一講解，我就懂了。

---

superior（adj.）優秀的
tough（adj.）棘手的、費勁的、艱難不順的

geometry（n.）幾何學
discouraged（adj.）灰心的、沮喪的
figure（v.）計算、估計、描繪

EVERYBODY can look back and recall classmates who were extremely good students. Of all my classmates in high school, Old Chang was the smartest one of all. But Old Chang was different than a lot of the superior students I knew, because he was always the type who was willing to help those of us who had a tough time in school. From Day One, the two of us were always in the same class section. Back then, geometry always left me feeling down and discouraged. I could never figure out when and how to add an auxiliary line. Usually we didn't bother much about our studies, until the time for exams drew near, that is. Then fear would begin to percolate inside us. Old Chang was always willing to step in as our voluntary private tutor. Our whole class would stay late on Saturday afternoons, and we'd listen intently as Old Chang would guide us through various problems and questions.

---

auxiliary（adj.）輔助的
draw near（ph.）接近、靠近
percolate（v.）滲透

voluntary（adj.）自願的
tutor（n.）家庭教師、私人教師
intently（adv.）專注地、熱切地

　　老張可以說是那種一帆風順的人，從小就有好的家庭，功課好，體格也很好，可是他一直關心他周遭比他不幸的人，他不僅一直都幫助功課不好的同學，也常常幫助家境不好的同學。大家畢業以後，老張事業不錯，但是他卻沒有很多財產，因為他一直捐錢給慈善團體，我們大家都知道老張是個大好人，卻沒有人想過為什麼他永遠有慈悲心，我們都認為他生來就是如此。

---

grasp（v.）領會、理解
tense（n.）（動詞的）時態、時式
explain（v.）解釋、說明

in good shape（adj.）身體健康的
fortunate（adj.）幸運的

He was a good English teacher. For the longest time, I just couldn't grasp the difference between the present perfect verb tense and the simple past tense. Actually, the only one who could get it in the whole class was Old Chang. He explained it and, presto, suddenly I understood.

Old Chang was the type of person who always had the wind at his back. From the time he was young, he had a good family and got good grades in school. He was in good shape, too. Yet Old Chang always took care of people around him who were less fortunate than he was. It wasn't that he only helped classmates who had a tough time in school. He helped those with family troubles too. Years after everybody graduated, Old Chang actually did pretty well in his business career, but he never accumulated much property. The reason was that he was forever donating money to charitable organiza-

---

accumulate（v.）累積、積聚　　charitable（adj）慈善的、寬容的
donate（v.）捐獻、捐贈　　　　organization（n.）組織、機構

老張還有一個特色。他會塗鴉，上課時會偷偷地畫老師，初中畢業，他送給每位同學一幅同學的畫像，都像是漫畫中的人物，表情都很誇張，看了令人啼笑皆非。

老張已經退休了，他的事業都已由專業人員接管，但他仍對於動畫有興趣。

有一天他打電話給我，邀我去參觀他一個電腦輔助

benevolent（adj.）仁慈的、有愛心的

caricature（n.）漫畫

sketch（v.）素描、塗鴉

tions. We all knew Old Chang was on all counts a remarkably benevolent human being, but none of us ever wondered why there was so much kindness in his heart. We imagined he was just born that way.

Another thing about Old Chang that was special was that he had a gift for drawing caricatures. During class he would secretly sketch pictures of our teachers. When we graduated from high school, he gave every classmate a portrait of themselves. The drawings all looked as if they had jumped out of a comic book, the expressions on our faces a bit exaggerated. No one knew whether to laugh or cry.

Old Chang is retired now, his business passed on to his managers beneath him. He has maintained his interest, however, in animated cartoon figures.

One day he called on the telephone and invited me

---

portrait (n.) 肖像　　　　　　　beneath (prep.) 在⋯⋯之下
exaggerated (adj.) 誇張的

動畫的軟體。這個軟體的確很有趣，是一種三度空間模型的動畫軟體。過去動畫中的人物是完全畫出來的，現在我們可以用一個三度空間的模型來描寫一個人物，這種方法的最大好處是有彈性，比方說，我們在動畫中有兩個大男人鬥劍，可以利用電腦技巧，一下子換成了一男一女鬥劍，當然也可以換成兩個女人在鬥劍。

我看到最有趣的是一位年輕人的特技表演，老張的軟體使這個年輕人忽然變成了蜘蛛人，一下子又變成了

animated（adj.）模擬有生命物體的
dimension（n.）維度、向度
literally（adv.）真正地、實在地

technique（n.）技巧、技術
dimensional（adj.）維度的、向度的
flexibility（n.）彈性、靈活性

to drop by to see some software he had developed for animated drawings on a computer screen. This software was truly something to behold. It presented models of figures in three dimensions, what is sometimes called "3D." In the past, animated drawings featured characters that were literally drawn by hand. Now there are special techniques to create three dimensional models for animated figures. The greatest advantages of this method are its flexibility and plasticity. Imagine we are watching two strong and husky male figures battling it out in a sword fight. Computer techniques allow us now to suddenly change one of the men into a sword wielding woman warrior. Of course we could also suddenly make it a clash between a pair of "sword women."

The most intriguing thing for me was seeing a young person performing magic acts. Old Chang's software allowed him to turn abruptly into a spider man. In a wink he became a batman. I asked Old Chang if he

plasticity（n.）可塑性、適應性、柔軟性
husky（adj.）高大健壯的
sword（n.）劍、刀
abruptly（adv.）突然地
wink（n.）瞬間、霎時

蝙蝠俠，我請他找一位老人的模型來試試看，他說當然可以，但是一定很可笑。果真如此，看到一個老頭子身手如此矯健，簡直是一場滑稽戲了。

我還看了一些動畫，有一個故事是有關於戰爭場面的，故事裡的軍人可以換成各個國家的。老張說他們正在建立一個資料庫，連背景也可以換掉，原來戰爭也許發生在歐洲，現在可以發生在亞洲，而且軍人也變成了我們亞洲人。

我看得津津有味，老張有一位部下忽然告訴我，說大老闆（指老張）畫了好多漫畫，而且保存在一張光碟裡。我對此大表興趣，向老張要來看，老張起初不肯，後來被我一再央求，終於給了我。

---

precisely（adv.）確實如此　　　　nimble（adj.）靈巧的、敏捷的
fogy（n.）守舊者　　　　　　　　lightning（adv.）閃電似地

could try out a model of an old man. "Of course," he replied, "but it'd make people laugh." In the end, that is precisely what he did. I saw an old fogy nimble on his toes and lightning quick with his hands. It was a hilarious scene.

I looked at still more of his animated drawings. One was a war story that had soldiers that could be changed into any nationality. Old Chang explained they were trying to create a data base, and could even change the background scenes. Perhaps originally the war broke out in Europe, but now it could be changed to Asia. The soldiers could become our own Asian people.

As I looked at all this, I became more and more enthralled. Old Chang had an assistant who mentioned his great boss (he pointed to Old Chang) had drawn many comics and as a matter of fact had put them into a DVD. I commented that I was quite interested in seeing

hilarious（adj.）極可笑的
nationality（n.）國籍

enthralled（adj.）被迷住、被吸引住

我帶了光碟回家，插入電腦，打開光碟，迎面而來的是四個大字，「我的故事」。顯然這些漫畫都是老張的故事了。

果真，這裡面全是一個一個故事，主人翁從小孩子開始，一直到大人，而且不論什麼時代，主人翁都很像老張，但是一望而知，故事都不是老張的故事，而且正好相反，這些都是老張絕對沒有經歷過的故事。第一個故事有關徐蚌大會戰。一個小孩子被迫由父母帶了逃難，他們在擁擠不堪的公路上行走了好久，終於到了火車站。在火車站，小孩子的爸爸走失了；火車進站，孩

relent（v.）心軟　　　　　　slip（v.）塞（入）、插入

that material. I asked Old Chang to let me look at it. At first he was unwilling to agree, but after I kept badgering him, he finally relented and gave me the DVD.

I took that DVD home. I slipped the disc into my computer and opened it. In large lettering, two words came to the screen: MY STORY. Apparently then, these cartoon figures would tell Old Chang's story.

Here is the way it turned out. Inside that disc was one story after the other. A child was the main character in the beginning, but he always grew up and reached adulthood. Also, regardless of what generation it might be, the main character always resembled Old Chang. Yet you knew as soon as you saw it that this was actually not Old Chang's story at all, and in fact was precisely the opposite. None of the contents whatever showed anything that Old Chang had personally gone through in his life.

---

resemble（v.）像、類似

子和媽媽擠上了火車,下了火車,馬上又走失了,只剩

下這孩子和他弟弟在上海街上流浪。

我知道老張生長在上海,共產黨佔領大陸的時候,

他們舉家來台,老張當然不是流浪街頭的小乞丐。這是

第一篇漫畫,畫的技巧比較幼稚,看來是老張小的時候

refugee（n.）難民、流亡者　　　　　Communist（n.）共產黨
promptly（adv.）很快地、迅速地

The first story was about the last battle the Kuomintang fought and lost against the Communist soldiers in the winter of 1948 and early 1949 in the areas of Xuzhou and Bangbu. That loss led to Chiang Kai-shek's flight to Taiwan. In Old Chang's story, a child and his mother and father are forced to flee as refugees. For a long time, they make their way along a very crowded road. Finally they reach the railway station, where the child's father promptly gets lost in the crowd. A train arrives at the station, and the children and mother enter one of the cars. When they get off the train later, however, they also find themselves separated in a great mass of people. The upshot of all this is that the child and his little brother are left to roam the streets of Shanghai.

I knew Old Chang was born and raised in Shanghai. When the Communists took control of mainland China, his whole family emigrated to Taiwan. Old Chang had obviously never been a beggar on the streets

---

emigrate（v.）移居　　　　　beggar（n.）乞丐

畫的。

　　以後的每一個故事都有同樣的主題和主人翁，主人翁永遠是一個很不幸的人物，比方說，有一則故事提到一個體育不好的中學生，每次上體育課以前都會肚子痛，可是體育老師一點也不同情他。

　　另一則故事是有關一位中學生輟學的事情。他功課不錯，但家境迫使他不能念高中，而要去做苦工，在烈日之下，拖著一輛裝冰的車子在台北行走，沒有想到碰到一批他當年的同學。那些學生都穿了高中制服，他卻

---

juvenile（adj.）未成熟的、幼稚的
woefully（adv.）悲哀地、令人遺

憾地
inadequate（adj.）不充分的、能力

of Shanghai.

That was the first animated cartoon story. The artistic techniques seemed a bit juvenile. Apparently Old Chang drew those figures when he was a child.

All the stories that followed featured the same themes and the same main character, who was forever a most unfortunate chap. One of the stories showed him as a woefully inadequate physical education student, for example. He had a stomachache before every PE class in high school, and his teacher didn't have an ounce of sympathy for him.

Another of the stories dealt with a high school drop-out situation. The protagonist does well enough in his classes, but his family circumstances make it impossible for him to go to senior high. He has to go out and find a job. It so happens one day that as he pulls an ice

---

不足的
sympathy（n.）同情

deal with（ph.）關於
protagonist（n.）主角

打了赤膊，他認出他們，他們卻沒有注意到他的存在。

我怎麼想都想不通為什麼這叫做「我的故事」，這實在應該叫做「不是我的故事」，因為老張的故事，正好是這些故事的相反。

我打了個電話給老張，他邀我到他家去坐坐，然後告訴我究竟是怎麼一回事。

老張小的時候，常吵著要媽媽帶他去看電影，當時二次世界大戰才結束，有很多歌頌戰爭的電影，老張當時是個小男孩，難免會對飛機有興趣，就去看一部叫做

---

uniform（n.）制服　　　　　roll（v.）翻轉；左思右想
stitch（n.）一件衣服（口語）　fathom（v.）推測、揣摩

cart along a street in Taipei, he bumps into a crowd of his old classmates. They are wearing their school uniforms, but he doesn't have a stitch on above his waist. He recognizes them, but they don't even know he exists.

Again and again I rolled this around in my mind, but I just could not fathom why he called this "My Story." The title truly ought to have been "Not My Story." Old Chang's story was the absolute opposite of these stories.

I called Old Chang on the telephone, and he invited me to come over to his house and sit down for a conversation. He would tell me what this was all about.

As a child, Old Chang would whimper until his mother agreed to his pleas to take him to a movie. World War II had recently ended, and there were a lot of movies that presented war as praiseworthy. Old Chang

---

truly（adv.）確切地
whimper（v.）哀哀叫

praiseworthy（adj.）值得稱讚的、可嘉的

《轟炸東京記》的電影。電影裡當然有彈如雨下的鏡頭，老張當時覺得這種炸彈落地，濃煙四處冒起的鏡頭很令他興奮，但他媽媽在旁邊提醒他，一定要記得地上是有人的。電影結束以後，他媽媽叫他好好地想像地上的老百姓遭遇到轟炸時的情況。

　　不久，內亂又起，老張上學的時候，發現滿街都是乞丐，後來他才知道，上海在短時間內湧入了超過一百萬的難民。有一天，他和一位小朋友在週日清晨的街上

---

entitle（v.）給（書等）題名　　　　descend（v.）下降
raindrop（n.）雨點、雨滴　　　　　imagine（v.）想像、猜想
bomb（n.）炸彈　　　　　　　　　situation（n.）處境、情況

was just a boy then, and had a natural interest in air planes. He saw a movie entitled *Diary of the Bombing of Tokyo*, and of course the film showed close-ups of bombs falling like raindrops from the sky. He felt greatly excited by the camera shots of the bombs descending through the air to the earth below, and of the thick dark smoke that billowed upwards from all sides. His mother, sitting beside him, reminded him that he should remember there were people on the ground. After the movie had ended, his mother told him to imagine what the situation was like for the common people down below and what they faced when a bomber flew overhead and dropped its payload

Not long afterwards, conditions became very chaotic. When Old Chang was still in school, he discovered the streets were full of beggars. Then came the time when he knew what it was like when, in a short span of

---

bomber（n.）轟炸機、投擲炸彈的　　chaotic（adj.）混亂的、雜亂無章
人　　　　　　　　　　　　　　　　的
payload（n.）炸藥

閒逛，眼看一個小乞丐死了，他的身體從台階上一路滾下來，他和他的朋友嚇得趕快跑回家去了。

　　老張當時已是小學生，可以看報，他從報上知道了徐蚌大會戰的事情。有兩張照片使他印象非常深刻，一張是公路上人山人海的難民潮照片，另一張是在火車站難民擠上火車的照片。他媽媽知道他在看報，又提醒他要設身處地地想「如果我也是一個難民，我會遭遇到什麼事呢？」

scamper（v.）跳跳蹦蹦、奔跑

days, wave after wave of refugees, more than a million all told, flowed into the streets of Shanghai. Early on a Sunday morning he was scampering about with a young buddy of his when their eyes fell upon a dead beggar-child. His body rolled right down a flight of steps leading into a building. In a state of shock, he and his little friend ran back home as fast as they could.

Old Chang was an elementary school student at the time, and he could read a newspaper, and it was from newspaper reports that he learned of that last Kuomintang-Communist soldiers battle around Xuzhou and Bangbu. Two photos made an especially deep impression on his mind. One showed great crowds of refugees, masses as big as oceans and mountains, as they slowly moved along the highways. Another photograph had huge groups of refugees jammed into a train at a railroad station. His mother, aware of his newspaper reading, reminded him to put himself in the place of others. "If I were a refugee, what conditions would I face?"

因為他從小就會塗鴉，他媽媽鼓勵他將所想到的畫下來，他也就畫出了第一篇漫畫故事，畫裡的主人翁是一個在戰爭被迫逃亡的小孩子。

終其一生，老張一直記得他媽媽的話「想想自己是一個不幸的人」，老張因此常常想像自己功課不好，自己體育不好，自己家境不好，這些想像也使得他心中充滿了慈悲心，絕大多數在良好環境中成長的孩子沒有什麼同情心的，因為他們很難想像有人會如此地不幸。老張媽媽的教訓，使他正好相反，他一直可以想像得到不幸的人會有怎樣的情境。

---

urge（v.）激勵 mediocre（adj.）中等的、平庸的
sketch（v.）畫草圖、素描

he asked himself.

From the time he was young, he could draw comics. Thus his mother urged him to let his drawings come from his imagination. That was when he sketched the first cartoon story. Its main character was a little boy who was forced to run for his life in a time of war.

So, all through his life, old Chang always kept in mind his mother's words. "Think of yourself as one of the unfortunate ones." So Old Chang always pictured himself as a mediocre student, or saw himself weak in Physical Education classes, or with a lousy family background. Using his imagination like that filled his heart with benevolence. The reason the great majority of children raised in ideal circumstances cannot feel sympathy for others is that they have such a difficult time imagining what it is like to suffer. Without a doubt, the lessons his mother taught to Old Chang helped him become very

---

benevolence（n.）仁慈、善心　　circumstance（n.）境況、境遇

　　老張還告訴我一件事，他的軟體在歐美賣得很好，因為有人將戰爭動畫給他的兒子看，兒子看了不太感動，這位父親將自己的兒子取代了動畫的主角，使兒子大受震撼，非常深刻地體會到戰爭的實境。他的軟體，好像一個虛擬實境，使人能親自體驗很多想不到的經驗。

　　老張給我看一個新完成的動畫──「推銷員之死」，很多美國人將自己取代了那位推銷員，看了以

miserable（adj.）痛苦的、不幸的　　virtual（adj.）虛擬的
jolt（n.）震驚

much the opposite of others. He could picture in his mind the miserable situations in which other people were thrown.

Something else Old Chang told me was that his software was selling well in Europe and the United States because when a father gave his computer-savvy son his animated war games to play with, if the son watched the characters but was not affected by them, the father could put the boy in the role of one of the characters. This would give the boy a real jolt, and impress him deeply about the reality of war. His software was like virtual reality, making things seem so realistic that you might forget that what you were looking at was imagined. The predicament of, say, a salesman, could be experienced personally by others through the software.

Old Chang let me see an animated cartoon program he had just completed called *"Death of a Salesman."* Many Americans had put themselves in the place of the

realistic（adj.）逼真的、寫實的　　predicament（n.）困境、窘境

後，會有意想不到的結果。

　　我在想，如果拿破崙在發動戰爭之前，有人給他一個戰爭的動畫，而那個在前線死掉的小兵是他的兒子，也許他就不會發動戰爭了。

　　我終於懂了，老張也不是生下來就對人充滿同情心的，他母親的諄諄教誨是慈悲心的根源。我們應該隨時默想世界上不幸同胞的遭遇，如果我們成天想到自己如何厲害，會越來越驕傲，越來越沒有同情心。如果我們成天假想自己非常不幸，我們就會變得謙卑而又有同情心。

　　　　　　——原載二○○五年五月十三日《聯合報·副刊》

---

casualty（n.）傷亡人員　　　　　encounter（v.）遭遇

main character there, and afterwards could feel in ways they had never thought possible.

I keep thinking that if someone had given Napoleon an animated cartoon program to watch before he went to war, and if he knew beforehand his sons were to be among the casualties, perhaps he would not have gone to battle.

In the end, I came to understand that Old Chang was not just born with a heart naturally full of sympathy. This was all due to his mother, whose earnest teaching and admonishments were the source of the goodness in his heart. The pain our unfortunate brothers and sisters encounter all over the world should always be in our hearts and minds. If all day long we think about how great we are, we become more and more proud of ourselves, and find less and less compassion in our hearts. If all day long we imagine how miserable we are, we will become humble, and develop hearts full of compassion.

---

compassion（n.）憐憫、同情　　humble（adj.）謙遜的、卑微的

特殊學生
A Special Student

鮑端磊　譯

我從小在希望與榮耀中成長，但我知道，世界上有數以億計的人，生命中沒有希望這兩個字。

From my childhood onward, I have grown up in hope and glory, but I know the world has millions and millions of people whose lives do not have that word "hope."

我們做老師的人，最害怕的是學生之中有問題學生，學生不用功，還有藥救，通常只要抓來罵罵就可以了，但是如果精神上有些問題，我們做老師的就手忙腳亂了。我沒有問題學生，但卻有一個特殊學生。

　　四年前，我接到一位中學老師的電話，他問我是不是吳台穎的導師，當時才剛開學，我還沒有和導生面談的機會，查了一下資料，發現我的新導生中，果真有這麼一位同學。這位老師是他的中學導師，所以他告訴了我很多有關吳同學的事，叫我特別注意他，因為他有些特殊。

profession（n.）行業、同行　　awry（adj.）歪曲、出錯
straighten（v.）改正、好轉　　guidance（n.）指導、引導
psychologically（adv.）心理上地

The one thing we in the teaching profession fear the most in a group of students is finding that one of them is "a problem student." There is always a way to save students who are not studious. Usually you pull them aside, say a few firm words, and they straighten themselves out. But if something is psychologically awry with a student, we teachers are at a loss. There is not a thing we can do. I have never had "a problem student," but I have had "a special student."

Four years ago, I received a telephone call from a high school teacher. He asked if I was the guidance counselor for a student named Wu Tai-ying. At the time we had just opened the new semester, and I hadn't yet had an opportunity to meet the students for whom I was to be a counselor. I checked my materials and, sure enough, found that among the students under my charge, this one was indeed on my list. This teacher was his high

---

counselor（n.）指導老師 opportunity（n.）機會、良機
semester（n.）半學年、一學期 material（n.）資料

　　因為這一通電話，我免不了對於吳台穎給予多多的注意，我發現他沒有任何一點的不同，他和其他的同學一樣，很好玩，上課時有時顯得沒精打采，但是一到了籃球場，精神就來了，第一次期中考，考得很不好，被我抓來罵一頓，以後功課就一直維持在前四名之內，週末也會和同學們騎機車出去玩。

　　吳台穎唯一特殊的地方是他的英文非常好，他說他

---

inevitably（adv.）不可避免地
certain（adj.）某種程度的
examination（n.）考試

scold（v.）責罵、斥責
performance（n.）成績、表現
fourth（adj.）第四的

school guidance counselor, and so he told me many things about this student named Wu. He told me to pay special attention to him because he was quite special.

Because of that telephone call, I inevitably paid a certain amount of attention to Wu Tai-ying. I found, however, there wasn't a speck of a difference about him. Like his classmates, he loved to enjoy himself. In class he sometimes seemed a little out of it, but when the time came to hit a basketball court, his spirits just jumped to life. He tested poorly the first time we had a mid-term examination. Once he was pulled over and scolded a bit by me, however, his school performance pushed him to his place as the fourth best student in his class. On weekends he enjoyed buzzing around on his motorbike with his classmates.

The only thing special about Wu Tai-ying was his extraordinary ability in English. He said from the time

---

motorbike（n.）摩托車　　　　　的
extraordinary（adj.）特別的、非凡　ability（n.）能力、才能

從小就不怕英文，什麼原因，他也說不上來。我知道他可以上網去看《紐約時報》，也會去看英國的《泰晤士報》，在暨南大學，他幾乎是絕無僅有的同學。

吳台穎一直在資工系系辦公室打工，他很勤快，早上來，會替花草澆水，也將桌椅擦一遍，所有進出系辦的老師們都喜歡他，一有事情，也會找他，主要理由是他永遠笑嘻嘻的。

資工系系辦的對面是資管系系辦，兩位系主任好像不常串門子，但是工讀生卻來往得很頻繁，互相妨害公務。資管系有一位很漂亮的女工讀生，吳台穎有事沒事

responsible（adj.）認真負責、可信賴的　　dust（v.）除去⋯⋯的灰塵　　furniture（n.）家具、設備

he was little, he had no fear of English. Whatever the reason for it, well, he couldn't quite put his finger on it. I knew he could read *The New York Times* and *The London Times* on the Internet. There was just nobody like him at Chi Nan University.

Wu Tai-ying had a working student's job in the office of the Information Science Department. He was very responsible. He came in the morning, watered the plants and dusted off the furniture and desktops. All the professors who came and went through the place liked him. Whatever their project might be, they wanted his help for it. The main reason is that he always wore a smile.

Across from the Information Science Department was the office for Information Management. It seemed as if the two department chairs rarely talked with one another, but the working students all knew each other.

---

desktop（n.）桌面
project（n.）計畫、方案、案子

across（adv.）在對面
rarely（adv.）很少、難得

就去資管系送公文，日久天長，就和那位工讀生變成情

人了。我曾經教過這位女生，知道她非常用功，因此鼓

勵吳同學去追。

　　有一天，吳台穎的女朋友來找我，她說吳台穎什麼

都好，只是有一件事，好像有點怪。因為他們已經交往

---

fraternize（v.）和樂地相處、相處　　deliver（v.）投遞、傳送
融洽　　　　　　　　　　　　　　　　eventually（adv.）最後、終於
obstacle（n.）妨礙　　　　　　　　　romantically（adv.）浪漫地、小說般地

Actually, those working students were forever bopping in and out of the offices, and it got to the point where all the fraternizing between them almost became an obstacle to getting any work done.

Information Management had a very attractive woman student doing work study service, and Wu Tai-ying found ways to go in there all the time to deliver paperwork of one kind or the other. He'd pull all the time he could to hang around in there. Eventually he and that working student became romantically involved. I had once taught the young woman in one of my courses, and knew she was a serious student. Therefore I encouraged Wu Tai-ying to pursue her.

One day, Wu's girlfriend came to see me. She said everything about Wu Tai-ying was quite excellent. There was just this one thing, and it seemed a little weird. The

involved（adj.）交往、相愛
pursue（v.）追求、向⋯⋯求愛

excellent（adj.）出色的、傑出的
weird（adj.）奇怪的、神秘的

超過兩年了，吳台穎去過她家，卻死都不肯讓她去見他的父母。她只知道他家在淡水，雖然遠了一點，仍去得成的。

　　我想起吳台穎是一個特殊學生，就請他來和我談談，吳台穎很機靈，他一進門就問是不是他女朋友來告狀了，我說是的，然後我直截了當地問他一個問題：「假如你的女朋友家境很不好，因此不願帶你去她家，她這樣做對嗎？」吳台穎想了一下，他說他會面對事實的。

---

adamantly（adv.）堅決地、固執地　　refuse（v.）拒絕、不肯

two of them had been a couple for more than two years, so Wu Tai-ying had visited her home. But he adamantly refused to let her meet his parents. She only knew his family lived in Tamshui. It was a bit far away, but surely was close enough to get to.

I thought, well this Wu Tai-ying is "a special student" alright, and so I'll just ask him to drop by for a little talk. Being as sharp as a tack, Wu took one step inside the door and said, "This is because my girlfriend came and talked with you?" I told him he had that right. Then I went right to the point by asking him a question.

"If there was something wrong with your girlfriend's parents or family, and for that reason she would never take you there to meet them, do you think this would be alright?"

Wu Tai-ying thought about it and said if that happened, he would find a way to deal with the situation.

situation（n.）情況、局面

不久，我在走廊上遇到吳台穎的女朋友，她告訴我她去淡水看吳台穎的父母，我問她他的家什麼樣子，她的回答是「不能談了」。

我仍然對吳台穎的家很好奇，但不好意思問他。他一定知道我的想法，有一天，我收到一片光碟，英文名字是"Hope and Glory"，意思是「希望和榮耀」。打開來看，原來是介紹吳台穎在淡水的家，是他自己做的。他的家的確特別，我只有在電影中看過這種優雅的豪宅，一進門一大片花園，花園中的一草一木，都是有人細心照顧的。他的家正面看上去只有一樓，但其實他的家一面對著花園，另一面倚山而建，面對的是淡水河的出海口，因為倚山而建，事實上卻是兩層。

hallway（n.）走廊、門廳
curious（adj.）好奇的、渴望知道的

embarrassed（adj.）窘的、尷尬的
introduction（n.）介紹
elegant（adj.）優美的、雅緻的

Not long after that, I met Wu Tai-ying's girlfriend in the hallway. She told me she had gone to Tamshui to meet Wu's parents. I asked her what his family was like, and her answer was, "I can't talk about it."

I was very curious about Wu's family, but felt too embarrassed to ask him anything. He clearly knew my thoughts. Then, one day I received a DVD. The English title was "Hope and Glory," the same meaning of the Chinese words for, well, "hope" and "glory."

I opened the DVD and watched it. In the beginning it was an introduction to Wu Tai-ying's family in Tamshui. He had filmed it himself, and his family certainly was special. Only in movies had I ever seen such an elegant mansion. One step into the front door and you were in the middle of a park, and in the park were grass and trees, all trimmed and perfectly manicured. The front of the house made it seem the structure had but

---

mansion（n.）宅第、豪宅　　　manicure（v.）將……修剪整齊
trim（v.）修整　　　　　　　structure（n.）建築物、構造

　　吳家的客廳當然用了整片落地的大玻璃，坐在沙發上，黃昏，可以看到夕陽西下的淡水河，晚上，可以看到對岸的燈火。更奇妙的是，這間客廳的另一面是鏡子，所以你如站在客廳裡，無論往哪一方向看，都可以看到淡水河。簡直比美凡爾賽宮裡的鏡宮。

　　吳台穎還介紹了他家的游泳池，原來他們家常年都

opposite（prep.）在……對面　　　　surround（v.）圍繞、包圍
harbor（n.）港灣、海港　　　　　　pane（n.）窗格、窗玻璃片
construction（n.）建造、建築物　　　dusk（n.）薄暮、黃昏

one floor, but actually the house was opposite the park. The other side was built up against the side of a mountain. Directly across was the Tamshui River, flowing out into the harbor. Because of the construction into the mountain side, the house actually had two floors.

The living room for the Wu family was naturally surrounded by great panes of glass. You could sit on a sofa at dusk and watch the sun as it sank down in the sky over the Tamshui River. At night you could see an array of sparkling lights on the opposite shore. And even more marvelously, no matter where you stood in the room, you could look into a mirror on the wall and see the Tamshui River. The view was comparable in beauty to the spectacular La Galerie des Glaces (Hall of Mirrors) in Chateau de Versailles in Paris.

Included in Wu Tai-ying's introduction was the family swimming pool. For a long time his family had a

---

array（n.）排列、陣列　　　　comparable（adj.）比得上
marvelously（adv.）妙極地、令人　spectacular（adj.）壯觀的、壯麗的
驚訝地

有一位專門的救生員。

　　在他們家的旁邊，有一棟比較小的房子，也非常漂亮，這是他們家的車庫和傭人住的地方，吳台穎在光碟中沒有說明他們家有幾輛汽車，也沒有說是什麼車子，但是他透露了一件事情，他們家最差的車子是Lexus。

　　光碟結束的時候，有以下的句子，「我從小在希望與榮耀中成長，但我知道，世界上有數以億計的人，生命中沒有希望這兩個字。」

　　我的特殊學生終於來找我了，他說他的爸爸曾經請最好的老師教他英文，也鼓勵他上網去瀏覽，他的爸爸認為這可以增加他的國際觀，將來對擴張爸爸的企業，

---

lifeguard（n.）救生員
garage（n.）車庫
servant（n.）僕人、傭人

quarter（n.）住處
mention（v.）提起、說起
slip（v.）不經意講出；透露

professional lifeguard on duty all year long.

Beside the house there was a smaller structure, also very beautiful. This was the family garage and servants' quarters. In the DVD Wu did not say clearly how many cars his family owned. Nor did he mention what kind of cars they were. But he let slip that the poorest vehicle was a Lexus.

At the conclusion of the DVD there were these words: "From my childhood onward, I have grown up in hope and glory, but I know the world has millions and millions of people whose lives do not have that word 'hope.'"

My "special student" finally came by to see me. He said his Dad had gotten him the best teachers he could find for English, and encouraged him to dive into the Internet to expand his knowledge. His Dad felt this

---

vehicle（n.）車輛
conclusion（n.）結尾、結束

dive（v.）探究、鑽研
expand（v.）擴張、增長

大有助益。沒有想到的是，他從此知道了世界上有多少
的窮人，那些非洲骨瘦如柴的飢民令他大吃一驚，也使
得他對他的豪華住宅感到羞恥，他無法接受這種奢侈生
活，更不願同學們知道他的家是什麼樣子。

吳台穎說他遲早要繼承這一大筆遺產的，他會將它
全數捐給窮人。我因此告訴他，有錢並不是什麼丟臉的
事，只要心裡有窮人，就是個窮人了。心中絲毫沒有想
到窮人，才是嚴重的事。

---

strengthen（v.）加強、增強
perspective（n.）觀點、視野
assistance（n.）援助、幫助
expand（v.）擴展、擴大

enterprise（n.）企業、公司
sink（v.）沉入、陷入
throe（n.）痛苦的掙扎
abject（adj.）自卑的、淒苦的

could strengthen his international perspective. This would all be of great assistance in expanding his father's business enterprises. No one ever expected this would enable him to discover just how many people were sunk in the throes of abject poverty. The gaunt masses of Africa, their bones almost sticking through their skin, shocked him. He was flooded with shame by the extravagant elegance of his own home. He simply could not accept this type of luxurious life, and by all means he wanted none of his classmates to know how his family lived.

Wu Tai-ying said he would someday inherit his father's money and property. He had decided to donate everything he owned to the poor.

I told him therefore that having money was no cause for losing face. Make your heart aware that poor

---

poverty（n.）貧窮、貧困
gaunt（adj.）枯瘦的、憔悴的
extravagant（adj.）奢侈的、浪費的

elegance（n.）精緻、優美、富麗
luxurious（adj.）奢侈的、豪華的
inherit（v.）繼承

　　吳台穎壓迫我寫一張字條給他，他叫我這樣寫的：
「吳台穎同學：你是一個窮人。李家同題」，我字雖不
好，仍替他寫了，他說他現在心情好多了。

　　臨走以前，他對我說「我不再是特殊學生了吧！」
原來他一直知道有些老師覺得他有些特殊。我點點頭，
表示同意。

　　不久，我忽然打他的手機，他問我什麼事，我告訴
他，我仍然認為他是一個很特殊的學生，他大概聽懂了
我的意思，因為他在電話的那一端笑得好快樂。

---

force（v.）強迫　　　　　　calligraphy（n.）書法、筆跡

people exist. In that way, you are with them. It would be a serious matter indeed if a person never gave a thought to the poor.

Wu Tai-ying forced me to write something on a piece of paper and give it to him. He had me write, "Student Wu Tai-ying, you are a poor person," and sign my name after the words. Although my Chinese calligraphy was not good looking, I still wrote the words for him. He told me he felt much better then.

Before he left, he said to me, "I am not a special student any longer!" He knew from the beginning that some teachers considered him special. I nodded my head to show I agreed.

Not long afterwards, I dialed his cell phone number. I said I still viewed him as a special student. He probably grasped my meaning because the laugh that

---

nod（v.）點頭　　　　　　　　grasp（v.）領會、理解

你如果碰到吳台穎，千萬不要對他說「恭喜發

財」。

——原載二○○三年六月三十日《聯合報・副刊》

---

float（v.）漂浮　　　　　　　　　　　prosperous（adj.）富有的、富足的

floated over the wires was so happy.

If you ever bump into Wu Tai-ying, whatever you do, don't say you hope he will be rich and prosperous.

麵包大師傅
My Baker

康士林　譯

　　李老師，你有好多博士學生，我卻只有國中畢業，你肯不肯承認我也是你的學生呢？

　　Professor Li, how many doctoral students do you have? I have only graduated from junior high school, are you willing to acknowledge me as one of your students?

我一直很喜歡好吃的麵包，清大門口有好幾家麵包店，我每家都去過，哪一家有哪一種好吃的麵包，我都知道。

最近幾個月來，有不知名的人送麵包給我。送的人是一位年輕人，我住的公寓管理員問他是誰，他不肯說，他說他的老闆是李老師的忠實讀者，風聞李老師喜歡吃麵包，所以就送來了。

這些麵包果真高級，就以法國麵包為例，送來的法國麵包非常地軟，可是皮都是棕色的，看上去好看，吃起來好香好軟，還有一種大型像蛋糕的麵包，也是相當地軟，口感奇佳，這種超軟麵包，有一層棕色的麵包

---

entrance（n.）門口、入口　　　　faithful（adj.）忠實的
anonymously（adv.）不具名地　　rumor（n.）傳聞
doorman（n.）看門人、警衛

I have always enjoyed eating bread. There are a number of bakeries near the entrance to Tsinghua University, and I have been to each one of them. I know what type of bread each one has.

In recent months, someone has been sending me bread anonymously. It was delivered by a young man. When the doorman of my apartment building asked the young man who he was, he was not willing to say. He only said that his boss was a faithful reader of mine, and that rumor has it that I like to eat bread, so his boss was sending it to me.

The bread being sent was really high class. Take the French bread as an example: it was very soft, but the crust was brownish so it looked very good, and it was so soft and had a great smell. How tasty to eat this soft bread. Then there was a large loaf of bread that was like cake. It too was fairly soft and left a wonderful taste in

---

crust（n.）麵包皮　　　　　　loaf（n.）（一條或一塊）麵包
brownish（adj.）呈褐色的　　　fairly（adv.）相當地

皮，上面撒滿了糖粉，可以切成一片一片來吃，裡面的
葡萄乾散佈得非常均勻。切成厚片，或是薄片，都一樣
好吃，我在全台灣各個麵包店去找，都沒有找到這種麵
包。

　　有一天，我開車回家，看到那一位年輕人。正要騎
機車離開，我偷偷地尾隨其後，好在他走的路沒有什麼
車子，我居然一路上都盯住了他，也找到了那家麵包
店。

　　我停了車，走出車子，迎面就是撲鼻而來的法國麵
包的香味，當時是下午五點半，也是通常法國麵包出爐
的時候。我進了店，正好看到一位大師傅拿了一大盤才

---

powdered（adj.）粉末（狀）的　　thick（adj.）厚的
raisin（n.）葡萄乾　　　　　　　thin（adj.）薄的
evenly（adv.）均勻地　　　　　　motorcycle（n.）摩托車
slice（v.）（食物）切成薄片　　secretly（adv.）背地裡、秘密地

the mouth. This super-soft bread also had a brownish crust on top of which was powdered sugar, and it was so good to eat. The raisins on the inside were distributed very evenly. It was good to eat no matter whether sliced thick or thin. In all of the bakeries in Taiwan that I had gone to look for this kind of bread, I had never found it.

One day, driving home from work, I saw that young man. He was leaving on his motorcycle so I secretly followed behind him. Fortunately there were not many cars on the road he took. Much to my surprise, I kept my eyes closely on him, so I did find the bakery.

When I stopped my car and got out, I was greeted with the sweet smell of French bread. It was 5:30 in the afternoon, just the time when the French bread was being taken out of the oven. Entering the bakery, I saw the head baker bringing a tray of bread out of the oven

---

fortunately（adv.）幸運地、僥倖地　　、傳入（耳中）
surprise（n.）驚奇、詫異　　　　　oven（n.）爐、灶、烤箱
greet（v.）迎面而來、映入（眼簾）　tray（n.）盤子、托盤

烤好的麵包出來上架。我猜他是大師傅，因為他身穿白衣，頭上還戴著一頂烘焙廚師專門戴的帽子，年紀很輕。

廚房門又打開了，這回送出來的，是法國麵包，我看到有人將這些新烤好的麵包，小心地包裝進一家印有某某大飯店的紙袋裡，顯然這些是要送到那家大飯店去的。果真，店門口有一輛來自那家大飯店的車子，正在等著接收這批麵包。

法國麵包運走了，大師傅忽然注意到我。他問我是不是李老師，我說是的，他說老闆關照，如果李老師來，就要接受特別照顧。他開了一扇門，叫我進去坐，我發現這間房間佈置得好舒服，各種布娃娃散在各地，

---

shelf（n.）架子　　　　　　　obviously（adv.）顯然地
kitchen（n.）廚房　　　　　　van（n.）小貨車
employee（n.）雇員、員工

and placing the bread on the shelf. I guessed he was the head baker because he was dressed in white and was wearing the kind of high hat worn by bakers. He was rather young.

The door to the kitchen opened again and this time it was the French bread being brought out. I saw an employee carefully putting this freshly baked bread in paper bags marked with the name of a certain large hotel. Obviously the bread was going to be sent there. Sure enough, at the entrance to the bakery there was a van from that hotel waiting for the bread.

After the French bread had been sent away, the head baker suddenly took notice of me, asking if I were Professor Li. I said that I was. He then said that the owner had given instructions that if Professor Li were ever to come, we were to give him special treatment. He opened a door, and asked me to go in and sit down.

suddenly（adv.）忽然
notice（n.）注意、查覺

instruction（n.）命令、指示
treatment（n.）對待、待遇

中間有一張小圓桌，桌子上鋪了印有碎花的桌布，也有

一瓶花，這位大師傅順手將花拿開，叫我等一下。我坐

在小圓桌旁邊，看到外面一棵樹的影子，正好斜斜地灑

在窗子上，這扇窗是有格子的那一種，窗簾是瑞士白

紗，看來這家店的老闆很有品味。

　　大師傅拿了一個銀盤子進來了，原來他準備了一套

下午茶來招待我。茶是約克夏紅茶，點心不是麵包，就

是餅乾。茶壺、杯子和盤子都是歐洲來的瓷器，我真想

拿起來看看是什麼牌子的。大師傅陪我一起享受，因為

這些食物才出爐，吃起來當然是滿口留香，但是大師傅

---

discover（v.）發現　　　　　　spread（v.）陳列、散佈

decorate（v.）裝飾、佈置　　　vase（n.）花瓶

comfortably（adv.）舒服地、舒適地　shadow（n.）影子

doll（n.）玩偶、洋娃娃　　　　panel（v.）加上窗格

I discovered that the room was decorated very comfortably. There were all kinds of baby dolls spread about, and a round table with a flowered table cloth in the middle of the room. On the table was a vase of flowers. The head baker took the flowers away and asked me to wait a second. Sitting at this small round table, I saw the shadow of a tree outside covering the window from one side. The window was paneled, and the curtains were white Swiss lace. It seemed that the owner of this shop had very good taste.

The head baker came in carrying a silver tray on which was the afternoon tea he had prepared for me. It was Yorkshire tea. The snacks were cookies and bread. The teapot and the cup and saucer were European chinaware. I really wanted to check to see what the brand was. The head baker joined me in this treat. Since everything was just out of the oven, it was of course scrump-

---

curtain（n.）窗簾、門廉
lace（n.）精緻的網織品
prepare（v.）準備
teapot（n.）茶壺

chinaware（n.）（總稱）瓷器
scrumptious（adj.）（口語）絕妙的、極好的

說，還有更精采的在後面。

　　精采的是什麼呢？是一種烤過的薄餅，捲起來的，裡面有餡，我一口咬下去，發現薄餅裡有餡的汁進去了，餡已經很好吃，因為餡汁進入了薄餅裡，餅本身也好吃得不得了，我問大師傅，這個餡究竟是什麼？他忽然賣起關子來，他說這是要保密的。可是他透露一件事，他幾乎每天都換餡，我雖然笨，也懂了，他用蔬菜和碎肉做餡，然後再放一些醬進去，我猜這些蔬菜，都是切得碎碎的，而且一定要有汁。他還告訴我一件事，他這一種餅是用炭烤的。他說不用炭烤，決不會如此之香，烤的時間不能太長，以防太多餡汁浸入薄餅，這樣餅就太軟了。

crepe（n.）烤薄餅
pancake（n.）薄煎餅、薄烤餅
filling（n.）（糕點的）餡

soak（v.）滲入、侵入
marvelous（adj.）（口語）妙極的、很棒的

tious. But the head baker said the best was yet to come.

Now what was the best? It was a crepe made of a very thin pancake that was rolled up and had a filling. I ate it in one bite and discovered that the juice of the filling had soaked through into the pancake. The filling was already great to eat, but the crepe was even better because of the juice of the filling in the pancake. This crepe was marvelous to eat. I asked the chief baker what the filling was. He wasn't willing to say and said it had to be kept a secret. But he did reveal one thing: he changed the filling almost each day. Although I'm on the stupid side, I still understood. He used vegetables and chopped meat for the filling and then added some sauce. I guessed that the vegetables were cut very finely and therefore certainly had some juice. He told me one more thing: this crepe was charcoal baked. If, he said, it had not been charcoal baked, it would indeed not smell so good. It could not be baked very long so as to prevent

---

reveal (v.) 透漏、揭露　　　　　charcoal (n.) 木炭
vegetable (n.) 蔬菜、青菜　　　　prevent (v.) 防止、預防
chop (v.) 切細、剁碎

　　當我在又吃又喝的時候，我聽到外面人聲嘈雜，原來大批食客也在享受每天出爐一次的烤捲餅。大師傅告訴他們，每天只出爐一次，現烤現賣，也不准外帶，因為這種餅冷了就不好吃了，每人只能買兩塊，但是老闆免費招待咖啡或紅茶，我都不敢問價錢，我想凡是免費招待茶或咖啡的食物，一定不會便宜。我看了一下這些食客，都是新竹科學園區工程師樣子的人，有一位還告訴別人，他吃了以後要趕回去加班，這些食客也很合作，吃了以後自動將店裡恢復得乾乾淨淨。

---

soak（v.）滲透
customer（n.）顧客、買主

batch（n.）一爐（烘出的麵包）；一批

too much of the juice from soaking the pancake, which would have made it too soft.

As I was eating and drinking, I heard people making noise in the next room. It was a large group of customers enjoying the daily batch of crepes that had just come out of the oven. The head baker was telling them that the rolls came out of the oven only once a day and were sold on the spot. They could not be taken out of the store because they were no good to be eaten cold. Each person could only buy two but the owner gave away free coffee or tea. I didn't dare ask the price because I knew that a dish that came with free tea or coffee would not be cheap.

I took a look at the customers. They all seemed to be engineer-types from the Hsinchu Science Park. One even was telling someone that after eating he had to rush back for work. These customers were so cooperative that

---

dare（v.）敢　　　　　　　　cooperative（adj.）樂意合作的

　　我對這家店的老闆感到十分好奇，就問大師傅能不能見到他，大師傅說他一定肯，叫我在一張沙發上休息一下，他去找老闆來。

　　老闆還沒有來，卻來了一個小夥子，他拿了一個大大的信封進來，說老闆要我看一下。我拆開信封，裡面全是算數的考卷，考的全是心算的題目，比方說，15×19，答案就寫在後面，學生不可以經過一般的乘法過程，而必須經由心算，直接算出答案出來。

　　我想起來了，十年前，我教過一個國小的學生，每

---

automatically（adv.）自動地　　　envelope（n.）信封
appear（v.）出現　　　　　　　　math（n.）數學

they automatically cleaned up the tables after they had finished.

I became more and more curious about the owner and asked the chief baker if I couldn't see him. He said that his boss was most willing to see me and told me to sit on the sofa for a second. He would go get his boss.

Before the owner came, a young fellow appeared bringing a very large envelope with him. The boss wanted me to take a look at something. I opened the envelope and on the inside were math examinations with questions that had to be answered using one's head. For instance, what is 15 x 19? The answer had to be written without writing down any calculations. You had to simply arrive at an answer doing the calculations in your head.

All of a sudden I remembered that ten years before

---

examination（n.）考試　　　　　calculation（n.）計算

一次教完了，他就要做心算習題，一開始他不太厲害，後來越來越厲害，數學成績也一直保持在九十五分左右，可惜得很，他小學畢業以後，就離開了新竹，我再也教不到他了。他家境十分不好，我也陸陸續續地聽到他不用功念書的消息。我雖然心急如焚，但鞭長莫及，毫無辦法。我曾經去看過他一次，還請他到一家飯館去飽餐一頓，那時他國一下學期。我勸他好好念書，至少不可以抽菸，不可以打架，不可以喝酒，不可以嚼檳榔。他都點點頭，說實話，我只記得他當時叛逆得很厲害，一副對我不理不睬的模樣。

---

tutor（v.）當……的教師
elementary school（n.）小學
capable（adj.）有能力的

accomplished（adj.）熟練的；能力強的
disappointment（n.）失望

I had tutored an elementary school student who, at the end of each of our classes, had to do such calculations in his head. He was not too capable at first but soon became more and more accomplished. His grade in mathematics always remained about 95. To my great disappointment, after he finished elementary school, he left Hsinchu. I had no chance to teach him again. His family situation was not at all good. Off and on I heard that he was not taking his studies seriously. Even though I was greatly concerned, there was nothing I could do since he was too far away for my exhortations. Nonetheless, I went to see him once and even invited him out to have dinner with me. He was then in the second semester of his first year in junior high school. I urged him to take his studies seriously. He should at least not be smoking, fighting, drinking or eating betel nut. He completely agreed, but, to be honest, I only remember him being very rebellious at that time. He looked to me as if he didn't understand a bit of what I

concerned（adj.）掛慮的、擔心的　　urge（v.）力勸
exhortation（n.）規勸、告誡　　betel nut（n.）檳榔
nonetheless（adv.）但是、仍然　　rebellious（adj.）造反的、叛逆的

　　這個孩子後來沒有升學，我聽到消息以後，曾經寫過一封信給他，第一勸他無論如何不要去ＫＴＶ做事，第二勸他一定要學一種技術，這樣將來才能在社會立足。我雖然寫了好幾封信給他，他卻都沒回。

　　就在我回憶往事的時候，老闆走進來了，原來大師傅就是老闆，也是我當年教過的學生。他說他進入國中以後，因為家境非常不好，不僅沒有錢補習，有時連學雜費和營養午餐費用都交不起，他知道他絕對考不上公立中學，也絕對念不起私立高中，只好放棄升學了。他很坦白地告訴我，他是很想念書的，但是家境不好，使他無法安心念書，有一次他跑進清華大學去玩，看見那

---

definitely（adv.）明確地、肯定地　　tuition（n.）學費

was saying.

Later on, he did not continue with his studies. When I heard this, I wrote him a letter. First I urged him no matter what not to work in a KTV. Secondly, I said that he definitely should learn a skill. Only in this way could he get his feet on the ground. Even though I wrote him a number of letters, I never got an answer back.

As I was remembering all of this, the owner walked over. As it turned out, the owner was none other than the chief baker, and he was the student I had at one time tutored. He told me that after he had entered junior high school, because his family's situation was extremely bad, he not only had no money to be tutored, but there were even times when he could not pay his tuition or lunch fees. He knew that there was no chance for him to enter a public high school, let alone a private school. All he could do was to give up on his schooling. He told me very frankly that he had really wanted to continue his

---

frankly（adv.）坦白地

些大學生，心裡好生羨慕，回家居然在夢中夢見自己成

了大學生，醒來大哭一場。

因為家境不好，後來又不想念書，他的確有一陣子

很自暴自棄，還好他的導師一直很關心他，他才沒有變

得太壞。但是國三的時候，眼見其他同學都在準備考高

中，他卻絲毫不管。表面上他假裝滿不在乎，心裡卻沮

喪得厲害。

就在這個時候，他收到我的信，他以為我會責備他

---

envious（adj.）羨慕的　　　　　afterward（s）（adv.）後來、以後
awake（v.）醒來　　　　　　　　self-destruction（n.）自毀；自暴自

studies but his poor family situation did not allow him to do so in good conscience. There was one time when he had entered Tsinghua University to kill time. When he saw all of those university students, he was so envious. That night at home he dreamed that he had become a university student; he started to cry when he awoke.

Because his family situation was not good, there was no way for him to continue his studies afterwards. Indeed, for a spell he was on the road to self-destruction, but fortunately his guidance counselor was very concerned about him, so as a result he didn't become too bad. But when he was in his third year of junior high school and saw before him all his classmates preparing for the entrance exam for senior high school, he didn't care one bit. That is, on the outside he pretended not to care, but on the inside, he was severely depressed.

It was at that time when he received my letter. He

棄
fortunately（adv.）幸運地、僥倖地

counselor（n.）指導老師

放棄升學的，沒有想到我一句責備的話都沒有，我只是鼓勵他要有一技之長，他想起我曾帶他去一家飯館吃飯，吃完以後在架子上買了一大批麵包送他，他到現在還記得那批麵包有多好吃。

國中還沒有畢業，他就跑去那家餐廳找工作。也是運氣好，他一下子就找到工作了，從此以後，除了當兵的幾年以外，他就一心一意地學做麵包，兩年前，他自己創業，開了這家麵包店。

他說他常常參加旅行團去國外旅遊，除了遊山玩水以外，他也注意外國人做麵包的技巧。他在俄國發現了俄國人大而圓的麵包實在好吃，也好看，可是不知向誰

---

criticize（v.）批評、非難、指摘　　　military（adj.）軍人的、軍隊的
fortunate（adj.）幸運的、僥倖的

thought that I would criticize him for not continuing his studies. Much to his surprise I didn't write a word of criticism. I only encouraged him to get a skill. He remembered that I had once taken him out to eat and afterwards had bought him a lot of bread. He still remembered how good that bread had tasted.

Even before finishing junior high school, he had gone to that restaurant where we had eaten to get work. He was quite fortunate and was given a job there. From then on, except when he was doing his military service, he was single-mindedly learning how to make bread. Two years before, he had set up his own business and opened his bakery.

He said he quite often took tours abroad. Besides enjoying the sights, he paid attention to how foreigners made bread. He learned that the big and round Russian loaf of bread was quite tasty but also pretty to look at,

---

attention（n.）注意、注意力　　　　foreigner（n.）外國人

拜師。後來他靈機一動到哈爾濱去拜師，那裡很多麵包店專門賣那些又大又圓的俄國麵包，那位大師傅知道他是遠從台灣來的，決定傾囊以授，所以他學會了做俄國麵包，前幾天有幾位俄國工程師來他的店，比手畫腳地讚美他的手藝。他在哈爾濱也學會了不少俄國菜，他說他過一陣子會請我吃他做的真正的羅宋湯。

　　至於烤捲餅，是他在土耳其學來的，在土耳其，這是街上小店裡供應的小吃，有錢人並不會對這種餅有什麼興趣，認為這種食味不登大雅之堂。他回來以後試

---

inspire（v.）激勵；啟示　　　　praise（v.）讚美、稱讚
engineer（n.）工程師、技師　　future（n.）未來、將來

but he didn't know whom to ask to teach him how to bake such a loaf. Later he was inspired to go to Harbin in China, which once had many Russians, and found a teacher there. There were many bakeries there that especially sold those big, round Russian loaves of bread. One baker, when he knew that he had come all the way from Taiwan, decided to teach him all the secrets. In this way, he learned how to make Russian bread. A couple days before a group of Russian engineers had come to his store and through finger language praised his baking skills. He had also learned how to cook a number of Russian dishes in Harbin. He said that he would sometime in the future invite me to have some of his authentic borscht.

As for his crepes, these had been learned in Turkey. They were a snack sold in a little shop on the street. Rich people were not interested in these and thought that the taste was not very elegant. When he was

authentic（adj.）真正的、道地的　　elegant（adj.）講究的、精緻的
borsch（t）（n.）羅宋湯

做，發現中式的餡最適合國人的口味。有一次他用雪裡蕻和碎肉放在餅上烤，吃過的人都讚不絕口。

他告訴我他今天的晚餐是法國麵包夾雪裡蕻肉絲，這也是他自己發明的，他帶我去他的廚房看他燒的湯，羊腿洋蔥湯，我當場弄了一碗喝掉，他說這是在新疆學來的，我從來沒有想到羊腿湯如此好喝，一點騷味都沒有。

我的學生雖然從來沒有回過我的信，卻始終對我未能忘情，他之所以不回信，是因為當時正好是青少年叛逆期。有一天他向他太太提起我，他太太建議他經常送

appropriate（adj.）適當的、恰當的　supper（n.）晚餐、晚飯
mustard green（n.）雪裡蕻　invention（n.）發明、創造

back in Taiwan, he discovered that a Chinese-style filling was most appropriate for the local taste. Once he put a kind of mustard green and chopped meat on the pancake and baked it. Those who tasted the results couldn't stop praising it.

He told me that for supper that evening the bread was French with mustard green and chopped meat. This was his own invention. He took me into the kitchen to show me the soup he was making: onion, leg of lamb soup. On the spot, I finished off a bowl of it. He said that he had learned how to cook this in the far west of China. I had never thought that leg of lamb soup could taste so good. There was no smelly taste to it.

Even though my student had never written back to me, he never was able to forget about me. That he didn't write back then was because he was still in his rebellious stage. One day he talked about me to his wife, and she

lamb (n.) 羊腿
soup (n.) 湯

rebellious (adj.) 造反的、叛逆的

麵包去給我。他也一直有一種預感，總有一天，我們兩人會見面的。

對我而言，這簡直是恍如隔世了，自從他畢業以後，我就和他失去了聯絡。我當然一直記掛他，怕他因為沒有念好書而三餐不繼。沒有想到他現在生活得如此之好。我當年勸他要學得一技隨身，他現在豈止一技隨身，他應該是絕技隨身了。

在我要離開以前，我又考了他幾題心算的題目，他都答對了。他送我上車的時候，問我：「李老師，你有好多博士學生，我卻只有國中畢業，你肯不肯承認我也是你的學生呢？」我告訴他，他當然是我的學生，而且將永遠是我的得意高徒，我只擔心他不把我當老師，畢

premonition（n.）預感、徵兆
graduate（v.）畢業
concerned（adj.）掛慮的、擔心的

hungry（adj.）飢餓的
acquire（v.）獲得、習得

suggested that he should send some bread to me. He had a premonition that one day we two would meet again.

This all seemed to me to be happening in another life. I had lost contact with him since he had graduated from elementary school. Of course I had been concerned about him all along, fearing that he might go hungry without enough schooling. It never occurred to me that he was leading such a wonderful life. I had advised him to learn a skill, and now he had acquired more than a skill. He had incomparable skills.

Before I left, I once again tested him on his skill in mental calculations. Each question he answered correctly. When he took me to my car, he asked, "Professor Li, how many doctoral students do you have? I have only graduated from junior high school, are you willing to acknowledge me as one of your students?" This is what I told him: "Of course you are my student. You are,

---

incomparable（adj.）無比的、無可
匹敵的

calculation（n.）計算
acknowledge（v.）承認

竟我只是他的家教老師而已。

　　他知道我將他看成我的學生，露出一臉燦爛的笑容。這個笑容帶給了我無比的溫暖。我其實什麼也沒有教他，只教了他兩件事，「不要學壞，總要有一技隨身」，沒有想到這兩句話如此有用。

　　　　　　──原載二○○三年十月三十一日《聯合報‧副刊》

---

moreover（adv.）並且、此外
recognize（v.）承認、認可、認定

beaming（adj.）笑容滿面的、笑逐
顏開的、燦爛的

moreover, the student who has satisfied me the most. My only fear is that you will not recognize me as your teacher, for I was only your tutor."

Knowing that I saw him as my student, he burst into a beaming smile, which gave me an incomparable feeling of warmth. I hadn't really taught him anything except for two things: "Don't become bad, and you need to have a skill." Never did I think that these two suggestions would have such a great effect.

---

skill（n.）技術、技藝

瑪利修女
Sister Mary

康士林　譯

　　其實我從來就弄不清楚生命的意義，但我知道如何過有意義的生活。這麼多年來，我一直扮演著好母親的角色，好多小孩子也因此有了母愛。

　　I really haven't any clear idea about the meaning of life, but I do know how to live a meaningful life. Over these many years, I have been playing the role of a good mother. In this way, many children have been able to have a mother's love.

老杜是我電機系的同學，他一直和我們不太一樣，我們念書都是應付考試的，老杜卻不同，他隨便念一下，就可以應付考試，所以他念書永遠念得非常徹底。我們選課的時候總是選容易的，他卻不然，在大學的時候，他就到數學系去選課，而且他也將電磁學念得非常好，遠遠比我們念得好。

　　老杜畢業以後，進了一家小公司做事，當時大家都熱中數位線路，只有他一個人做的是類比線路，我們都覺得他有點頭腦不清楚。沒有想到的是，多媒體電腦來臨以後，他練好的功夫大為有用，全國會設計類比電路

---

electrical（adj.）與電有關的
engineering（n.）工程學
department（n.）（大學的）系
thorough（adj.）徹底的

select（v.）選擇、挑選
college（n.）大學、學院
electromagnetics（n.）電磁學

My old friend Du was a classmate of mine in the Electrical Engineering Department. All along he was much different from us. When we were studying, we all had to deal with exams, except for Du. He only had to take a quick look at the book and then could deal with the exam. And so he was ever very thorough in his studies. When we selected our classes, we always decided to take the easy ones, but he did not. In college, he would even go to the mathematics department for class. Further, he was very strong in the study of electromagnetics. By far he was a better student than we were.

After graduation, Du worked in a small company. At that time, digital circuits were hot items, and Du alone did analogue circuits. We all felt that he was a bit off. But much to our surprise, once multimedia computers were launched what he had learned so well had much use. In all of Taiwan, there were very few who had the

---

graduation（n.）畢業　　　　　　　analogue（adj.）類比的
digital（adj.）數字的、數位的　　　multimedia（n.）多媒體
circuit（n.）電路、回路、線路圖　　launch（v.）開始

的人非常少，他也自己開了公司，公司的股票一漲再漲，老杜的身價也一漲再漲。我們都非常羨慕老杜，總覺得老杜為什麼如此聰明，無論做什麼事，都做得這麼好。

可是我們大家卻有一種奇怪的感覺，那就是老杜不是那種以賺錢為唯一目的的人。不論他賺多少錢，他不會因為他賺了這麼多錢就心滿意足了。

過一陣子，老杜開始追求別的東西了，他常常出國，但出國不是在於推廣公司的業務，而是為了追求一些精神上的滿足，他常到各種靜修的地方去，照他講，他到的地方都是有名的地方，也常常聽到有名的宗教領

---

stock（n.）股票
envious（adj.）羨慕
strange（adj.）奇怪的
purpose（n.）目的

completely（adv.）完全地
satisfied（adj.）感到滿意
attention（n.）注意力
abroad（adv.）到國外

ability to design analogue circuits. Du then opened his own company, and its stock went higher and higher, as did Du's own worth. We were very envious. How could he be so smart? No matter what he did, it was always good like this.

Still we all had the strange feeling that Du was not someone for whom making money was the only purpose in life. No matter how much money he made, he never seemed to be completely satisfied just because he had made a lot of money.

As time passed, Du started to pay attention to other things. He often went abroad, but it was never to promote his company's affairs. His trips were to seek spiritual satisfaction. He often went to places for a spiritual retreat. To hear him talk, the places he went to were famous, and he often heard famous religious leaders

---

promote（v.）宣傳、推銷　　　　satisfaction（n.）滿足
affair（n.）業務　　　　　　　　retreat（n.）靜修、修養所
spiritual（adj.）精神的、心靈的　religious（adj.）宗教的

袖講道，可是他一直對這些講道不太滿意。他常常覺得
這些高僧講的道，不是聽不懂，就是了無新意。

老杜所想要得到的是生命究竟有何意義。我們這些
學電機的人當然幫不上忙，他老兄花了好多錢去探索生
命的意義，也常以靜坐的方式去悟出生命的意義，照他
講，他是越悟越糊塗。

有一天，老杜忽然打電話給我，平時他講話向來是
痛痛快快，這次他卻欲言又止，原來他說他要去找一位
他過去的一個女性朋友，這位女性朋友姓張，老杜在大
學時參加過山地服務社，就在那時候他認識張小姐，也

---

preach（v.）講道、佈道　　　　investigate（v.）調查、研究
eminent（adj.）著名的、卓越的　practice（v.）實行、實踐
monk（n.）修道士　　　　　　　meditation（n.）冥想、沉思

preach. He was never satisfied, however, with their preaching. He often felt that when these eminent monks were preaching, he either did not understand or that they had nothing new to say.

What Du was looking for was the very meaning of life. We who had studied Electrical Engineering of course could not help. The guy spent so much money investigating the meaning of life. He often practiced sitting meditation to seek enlightenment about the meaning of life but, according to him, the more enlightened he became, the more confused he was.

One day Du called me all of a sudden. Ordinarily his talk was always direct and to the point but this time he was rather reserved and hesitant. The upshot of the call was that he was going to see an old female friend of his by the name of Zhang. In college, Du had taken part

---

enlightenment（n.）啟蒙、頓悟
confused（adj.）困惑的、惶惑的
ordinarily（adv.）平常地、慣常地

reserved（adj.）有所保留的
hesitant（adj.）遲疑的、躊躇的
upshot（n.）重點、結果

有些來往，雖然我們不能說張小姐是老杜的女朋友，但是人人都知道老杜非常心儀張小姐的。

　　大學畢業以後，老杜告訴了我們一個令他心碎的消息，張小姐決定去做天主教修女了，她參加的組織專門替原住民服務。老杜雖然有失落感，當然也很佩服她，張修女發終身大願的時候，老杜曾經去觀禮，他站得遠遠地觀看了全部的儀式，事後就永遠不再提張小姐了，畢竟人家已經是修女了。

　　這次老杜告訴我，他終於找到了張修女，她在好遠的山地村落替一群小孩子服務。這些小孩子家裡發生了一些變故，張修女在照顧他們。老杜說，這二十年來，

volunteer（adj.）自願參加的　　　　nun（n.）修女
develop（v.）發展　　　　　　　　congregation（n.）宗教團體
relationship（n.）關係　　　　　　exclusively（adv.）專門地

in volunteer work up in the mountains and had met Ms. Zhang then. They developed a kind of relationship but it could not be said that she was his girlfriend; everyone just knew that he especially liked her.

After graduation from college, Du told us some news that had left him heartbroken. Ms. Zhang had decided to become a nun whose congregation worked exclusively for the Taiwan aborigines. Although he was disappointed, he still admired her decision. When Sister Zhang took her final vows, Du went to the ceremony. Standing far in the back of the church, he followed the entire ceremony. Afterwards, he never again mentioned Ms. Zhang, for now she had become a nun.

During this call, Du told me that he had finally found Sister Zhang. She was working with a group of children in a mountain village very far away. Sister Zhang was taking care of these children, because some-

---

aborigines（n.）原住民　　　vow（n.）誓言
disappointed（adj.）失望的　　ceremony（n.）儀式、典禮
admire（v.）尊敬、景仰、崇拜　mention（v.）提起、說到

張修女從未離開過那個山地小村莊，她一定會告訴他生命的意義何在。

我同意他的看法，可是我不懂為什麼老杜要告訴我這件事情。原來老杜想去看她，但不敢一個人去，他要我陪他一起去，替他壯膽。老杜已經四十幾歲的人，一夜之間，變成了小孩子，也難怪他，誰敢去找一位修女呢？

我們兩個人開了車，終於找到了張修女工作的地方，一進去，迎面而來的就是一些鬧得不可開交的小孩，那裡有好幾位修女，我們問了一陣子，找到了張修女。張修女看到我們，很和氣地問我們來的目的。我們

---

observation（n.）言論、意見　　　moral（adj.）道義上的；精神上的
accompany（v.）陪同、伴隨

thing had happened in their families. Du told me that Sister Zhang had not left that mountain village for these twenty years. She could tell him where to find the meaning of life.

I agreed with his observation, but I couldn't understand why Du had told me this. Then I realized that he wanted to see her but did not dare to go by himself. He needed me to accompany him and to give him moral support. Du was already over forty but overnight he had become a child again. But who could blame him? Would anyone in their right mind go look for a nun.

The two of us went by car, and at last found the place where Sister Zhang was working. When we entered, we were welcomed by a rambunctious group of kids. There were also a number of Sisters there. After making inquiries, we found Sister Zhang. When she saw us, she very kindly asked us why we had come. We said

---

rambunctious（adj.）喧鬧的　　　　inquiriy（n.）詢問、打聽

說我們是來捐錢的，於是張修女就帶我們去她的辦公室。到了辦公室，老杜再也按捺不住，他告訴張修女他的名字。

張修女聽到老杜的名字，大吃一驚。她說她完全沒有想到他會來這麼偏遠的地方。她雖然在這二十年來，從沒見過老杜，卻在報紙上常常看到這位電子新貴的消息。她說她常常替他祈禱，但是她沒有說她祈禱的意向，我猜這絕對和賺錢無關。

張修女卻不是一個閒人，那些調皮的小孩子不停地去告狀。一個小女孩說一個小男孩偷吃了她的餅乾，張修女給她一塊新的，卻引起一大堆小孩子都來要餅乾。一個小男孩摔了一跤，哭著來找張修女。張修女將他抱

---

donation（n.）捐款　　　　　pray（v.）祈禱
restrain（v.）抑制　　　　　reveal（v.）透露

we had come to make a donation, so she took us to her office. In the office, Du could not restrain himself any more, and told Sister Zhang his name.

Sister Zhang was greatly surprised when she heard Du's name. She had never imagined that he would come to such a far-away place. Although she had not seen Du for these twenty years, she had often read news of him, one of those very successful engineers, in the newspaper. She said that she often prayed for him, but did not reveal the intention of her prayers. I guessed that it had nothing to do with making money.

Sister Zhang, however, was not a person without things to do. Mischievous children kept coming in to report on others. A little girl claimed that a boy had eaten her cookie. Sister Zhang gave her another one, and that made a gang of children rush in wanting cookies. A little boy had fallen down, and came crying to Sister

---

intention（n.）意向、目的　　　claim（v.）聲稱
mischievous（adj.）調皮的、淘氣　gang（n）一群、一夥

了一陣子，他才不哭了。

　　就在這種紛紛擾擾的情況之下，老杜向張修女說他
這幾年來一直在尋找生命的意義，但一直搞不出所以
然，他相信張修女一定知道答案。

　　張修女的答案才真令我們大失所望，她說她其實是
一個很沒有學問的修女，對於神學知道得少之又少，如
果硬要說明生命的意義，她可以去查書，但她相信書上
的答案，老杜早就知道了，也不會使他滿意的。她還調
皮地問老杜，如果像他這麼聰明的人都無法了解生命的
意義，誰能了解呢？

spell（n.）一段時間　　　　　explanation（n.）說明、解釋
chaotic（adj.）混亂的、無秩序的　disappointed（adj.）失望的
circumstance（n.）情況

Zhang. He only stopped crying after she held him in her arms for a spell.

In was under these chaotic circumstances that Du told Sister Zhang that he had been looking for the meaning of life all of these years but he could never find any explanation. He was sure that she knew the answer.

Her answer, however, left us greatly disappointed. She said that she was a Sister without any scholarly knowledge. She only knew a very, very little about theology. If we really wanted her to explain the meaning of life, she could go look it up in a book. But she was sure that Du already knew the answer found in a book and that it would not be satisfactory for him. She then playfully asked him that if someone as intelligent as he could not understand the meaning of life, then who could.

---

scholarly（adj.）學問精深的
theology（n.）神學

satisfactory（adj.）令人滿意的
intelligent（adj.）聰明的

就在張修女和我們聊天的時候，另一位修女來了，她暗示廚房在等她燒飯。我和老杜到了這個時候，已經餓得發昏。之前小朋友拿餅乾的時候，我們兩人也分到了一些。不過這實在不夠，我們也知道附近沒有什麼飯店，要想吃飯，定要隨著張修女進廚房去。

一進了廚房，張修女就給了我們每人一件圍裙，我們立刻想起了「天下沒有白吃的午餐」的意義。

要燒一頓飯給幾十個人吃，儘管多數是小孩子，當然也不是易事。我們兩個手忙腳亂地幫忙，等到飯菜上桌，我們又被分派去不同的桌子管小孩吃飯，因為這兩桌的原來老師正好休假。這些小孩發現有客人來，紛紛

---

hint（v.）暗示　　　　　　　apron（n.）圍裙
famished（adj.）非常飢餓的

As we were talking with Sister Zhang, another Sister came over. She hinted that Sister Zhang was needed in the kitchen to cook. By this time Du and I were famished. Earlier when the kids had come for cookies, we were given our share too. But this was not enough. We knew that there was no restaurant nearby and that if we wanted to eat we needed to follow Sister Zhang to the kitchen.

Once in the kitchen, Sister Zhang gave each of us an apron. We then immediately thought of the expression "There are no free lunches."

To cook for twenty or thirty people is no easy thing even if most of them are kids. The two of us clumsily lent a helping hand. Once the food was on the table, we were then sent to different tables to look after the kids as they ate, since the teachers who would have been at the two tables were off. Once the kids discovered that

---

immediately（adv.）立即　　　　discover（v.）發現

發起人來瘋，有一個小孩，每一口飯都要老杜餵他，有一位修女來指責他，老杜卻替他辯護，他一方面胃口奇佳，一方面被這些小孩鬧得快樂無比。

吃完飯，我們兩人以為可以休息了，沒有想到張修女命令我們帶孩子們去睡午覺，這些小孩子一點也不怕我們兩個人，我們花了九牛二虎之力，才將這些孩子哄睡著了。

張修女在她的辦公室裡再度招待我們，也倒了茶給我們喝，老杜喝了茶以後，向張修女說：「我現在懂得妳為什麼二十年來沒有離開這個工作了，妳這樣的生活的確是有意義的。」

---

insist（v.）堅持、一定要　　mouthful（n.）一口
feed（v.）餵（養）　　　　reprimand（v.）訓斥、斥責

there were guests, they started to act crazy. One kid insisted that Du feed him mouthful by mouthful. A Sister came over and reprimanded the kid, but Du defended him. On the one hand, Du was satisfying his hunger, and, on the other, was being made incomparably happy by the kids.

After eating, the two of us thought we could rest. We never imagined that Sister Zhang would order us to take the children for their afternoon nap. The kids did not fear the two of us at all. We had to use all of our brute strength to get them to sleep.

Sister Zhang then once again entertained us in her office, giving us tea to drink. After taking some tea, Du said, "I now understand why you have not left your work for these twenty years. This kind of life really has meaning for you."

---

hunger（n.）飢餓　　　　　　　nap（n.）小睡
incomparably（adv.）無比地　　brute（adj.）野蠻的

　　修女點點頭，她說：「其實我從來就弄不清楚生命的意義，但我知道如何過有意義的生活。這麼多年來，我一直扮演著好母親的角色，好多小孩子也因此有了母愛。任何人只要肯全心全意地去幫助別人，都會感到自己的生活是有意義的。生命的意義也許難懂，要過有意義的生活，卻不是難事。」

　　老杜點點頭，他說在替那個撒嬌小孩餵飯的時候，他覺得他活得好有意義，至於生命的意義是什麼，他大概從此不想去研究了。他從此要過有意義的生活。

　　張修女說她知道老杜是一個聰明的人，他一定能夠

---

nod（v.）點（頭）　　　　entire（adj.）全部的
role（n.）角色　　　　　　perhaps（adv.）或許

Sister Zhang nodded her head in agreement and said, "I really haven't any clear idea about the meaning of life, but I do know how to live a meaningful life. Over these many years, I have been playing the role of a good mother. In this way, many children have been able to have a mother's love. We only have to help other people with our entire self and then we will be able to realize that our life has meaning. The meaning of life is perhaps difficult to understand, but to live a meaningful life is not that hard."

Du now nodded his head in agreement and said that as he was feeding that pouting little child, he felt that his life certainly had meaning. As to what is the meaning of life, he probably did not have to go to study any more. From now on, he would live a meaningful life.

Sister Zhang said that she knew Du was an intelli-

---

difficult（adj.）困難的　　　　　pout（v.）嘟嘴生氣
meaningful（adj.）有意義的　　　certainly（adv.）確實

領悟如何過有意義的生活，所以她沒有講什麼大道理，

僅僅將他拖下水。讓他嚐嚐幫助別人的快樂，果真老杜

很快領悟了。

　　我們要告辭的時候，張修女找到了一盒伯爵紅茶送

給老杜，她說她記得老杜在大學生時代很想喝伯爵紅

茶，可是沒有錢買來喝。當時她家比較有錢，有時還請

他。可是現在她不能喝這種昂貴的紅茶，因為她已經沒

有任何收入，喝不起這種奢侈品。她告訴老杜，自從畢

業以來，她沒有賺過一毛錢。

　　老杜收了伯爵紅茶，脫口而出，「小雲，謝謝妳。」

小雲顯然是張修女的名字，張修女只好告訴他，她早已

---

doctrine（n.）理論學說　　　　expensive（adj.）昂貴的
afford（v.）買得起　　　　　　salary（n.）薪資

gent person. He would certainly be able to understand how to live a meaningful life. Therefore, she had no special doctrine to teach him, she could only give him something to do. She would let him experience the joy of helping others, and he would quickly come to a full understanding.

When we were saying good-bye, Sister Zhang found a box of Earl Grey tea to give to Du. She said that she remembered that in college Du had wanted to drink Earl Grey tea, but could not afford it. Since her family was fairly well off, she would sometimes invite him to have some. But now she could not drink such expensive tea, because she did not have any salary at all. She could not afford such a luxurious thing. She told Du that since graduation she had not earned a single penny.

Du took the Earl Grey tea, and blurted, "Xiaoyun, thank you." Xiaoyun was obviously Sister Zhang's original name. Sister Zhang could only tell him that she did

---

luxurious（adj.）奢侈的　　　　blurt（v.）衝口説出
penny（n.）一文錢　　　　　　obviously（adv.）顯然地

不用這個名字了，在這裡，她是「瑪利修女」。

老杜發動車子以後，向車子外面的張修女說：「瑪利修女再見！我會過有意義的生活的！」

這是二十年前的事，老杜在台北從此一直照顧一批家遭變故的小孩子。我有一次看到老杜帶著一個小男孩去買夾克，我也曾經見到他請幾個小孩子吃飯。他最厲害的一點是能教一些高職生電機。儘管他的事業非常成功，他從未停止這種工作。

而我呢？我二十年前在德蘭中心開始做義工。我的教書生涯應該算是很順利的。做到了大學校長，也得到

misfortune（n.）不幸的事　　的；了不起的
impressive（adj.）予人印象深刻

not use this name any more. Here she is known as "Sister Mary."

Du started the engine and said to Sister Zhang who was standing beside the car, "Good-bye, Sister Mary. I will live a meaningful life."

All of this had happened twenty years ago. Afterwards, in Taipei, Du looked after a group of children whose families had had some misfortune. I once saw him taking a little boy to buy a jacket. I also once saw him taking some children out to eat. The really impressive thing that he did was to teach electrical engineering to some vocational high school students. Even though his business was very successful, he never stopped this kind of work.

As for me? I started doing volunteer work at the Theresian Center twenty years ago. My academic life

---

vocational（adj.）職業的　　　　academic（adj.）學術的

了好多學術界不易得到的獎項，但我總覺得我的生活之

所以有意義，是因為我一直在幫助不幸的孩子們。

　　我們兩人都已是六十五歲，頭髮雖白，但仍健在，

瑪利修女卻已在前些日子離開了人世，去世之前，她一

直在鄉下一家小醫院接受治療，有人建議她轉診到台北

的大醫院，她拒絕了。她說對世界上絕大多數人來說，

這種大醫院是奢侈品，她不願意享受這種奢侈品。她去

世之前，也有一些令她記掛的事，都是有關孩子的事，

某某孩子扁桃腺發炎，某某孩子手臂開刀，有一個國中

畢業的男孩子到台中去找工作，一直找不到，後來打電

話來，他找到了隨車送貨的工作，修女聽到了以後，安

心地閉上眼睛，從此沒有再醒過來。

---

unfortunate（adj.）不幸的　　　　　despite（prep.）儘管

could be considered to be fairly successful. I even became the president of a university and received awards that many in academics do not easily get. But I always felt that why my life has meaning is because I have never stopped helping unfortunate children.

Du and I are now sixty-five years old. We're healthy despite our grey hair. Sister Mary passed away a few days ago. Before her death, she was receiving treatment at a small hospital in the countryside. It was suggested that she should go to a big hospital in Taipei, but she refused. She said that for most people in the world, such a big hospital is a luxury. She was not willing to enjoy such a luxury. There were also some things that worried her very much before her death. They were all about children. One child had tonsillitis. Another had an operation on his arm. There was a boy who had graduated from junior high school who had gone to Taichung to look for work and couldn't find any. Later he called her and said that he had found work as a delivery boy. After Sister heard this, she peacefully closed her eyes and

tonsillitis（n.）扁桃腺炎

　　我們當然都去參加了瑪利修女的葬禮。彌撒開始，前面的座位是空著的，在合唱聲中，一百多位瑪利修女照顧的孩子們兩個一排地走了進來。我從未聽過如此好聽的聖歌大合唱。當修女的棺木離開教堂的時候，一個小男孩好大聲地哭喊：「瑪利修女，不要走！」

　　我們兩人不約而同地想起了瑪利修女所說的話，「我不懂生命的意義」。其實她是懂的，她知道生命的意義是無法用文字詮釋的，她選了另一種方法來詮釋她的想法，她將她的一生過得非常有意義，「有意義的生活」應該是「生命的意義」最好的詮釋了。

　　　　　　——原載二○○四年二月三日《聯合報・副刊》

---

funeral（n.）葬禮　　　　　　pew（n.）教堂內的靠背長椅

never awoke again.

We all went to the funeral of Sister Zhang. As the Mass started, all of the pews in front were empty. Then, with the sound of singing voices, over one hundred children who had been cared for by Sister Zhang entered two by two. I had never heard such a wonderful-sounding choir before. As her casket was being taken from the church, a little boy cried out, "Sister Mary, please do not leave."

Du and I both thought of what Sister Mary had told us: "I do not understand the meaning of life." In fact, however, she really did. She knew that the meaning of life could not be expressed in words. She had selected another way to express life's meaning, and she had led a very meaningful life. "A meaningful life" is the best explanation of "the meaning of life."

---

choir（n.）唱詩班　　　　　　casket（n.）棺材

是我應該謝謝你
It Is I Who Ought to Thank You

鮑端磊　譯

　　這種不幸的人一定早已存在的，只是他的世界中，沒有這種人，也許他曾經在街上看到過，但是他對這種人毫不關心⋯⋯

This type of unfortunate person surely had existed long ago. It was just that his world didn't have anyone like that. Perhaps he had seen people like this on the street, but he hardly ever cared about them...

陳董事長上星期在我們醫院裡逝世了，葬禮也已舉行。但是，昨天他的兒子打電話給我，說有些問題要問我，我們約好了在一家咖啡館見面。

陳董事長在我們醫院裡住了兩個月，他這種人當然有一本記事本，重要的事情會進入這本冊子，陳先生的兒子和我見面的時候，他給我看的就是陳先生的記事本。

這本記事本上所記錄的資料大多是陳先生在他的事業上所做的決定，包含如何發股份，如何發行公司債等等。但是在陳先生去世前的一個月，記事本裡出現很多

---

conduct（v.）實施、處理
appointment（n.）約會
patient（n.）病人

certainly（adv.）當然、確實
jot（v.）草草記下
content（n.）內容

A GENTLEMAN NAMED CHEN, who had been a Chairman of the Board, passed away last week at our hospital. His memorial service has already been conducted. Yesterday, however, I received a telephone call from his son. He said he had a few questions for me, and we made an appointment to meet at a coffee shop.

Chairman Chen was a patient at our hospital for two months. This is the type of person who certainly kept a notebook, and important matters were sure to be jotted down in those pages. When Mr. Chen's son and I met, he had me take a look at the elderly Chen's notebook.

Most of the contents of that notebook involved details of decisions Mr. Chen had made for his professional duties and business dealings. He'd left a record of directives on how to handle his company's holdings, how

---

involve（v.）與……有關
decision（n.）決定、決策

professional（adj.）職業的、很內行的

令人困惑的句子。陳先生的兒子用紅筆勾了以下的幾個

句子：

　　我願意。

　　我終於見到了。

　　是我應該感謝你。

　　如果他要來，誰都擋不了的。

　　這些話的確看起來很令人丈二金剛摸不著頭腦，可
是我慢慢地想起來了，這中間所發生的事，是很神祕
的。

---

issue（v.）發行、配給　　　　phrase（n.）片語、詞語
debenture（n.）銀行證券　　　incident（n.）事件、插曲

to issue debentures, and so on. Written during the final month of Mr. Chen's life, however, were several sentences that really made you stop and wonder. In red ink, his son had drawn check marks beside some of the phrases.

I want to... Now I can finally see... It is I who ought to thank you... If he wants to come, who can possibly stop him?

No doubt about it, words like that will ring bells like clanging gongs and make a fellow's head spin in circles. But slowly I became aware of a few incidents that had occurred during those last days of his. Some mysterious things did happen.

---

mysterious（adj.）神秘的、不可思議的

　　陳董事長住的病房，是醫院的超級特等病房，有好幾間房間，病房佈置得像臥室，除了臥房以外，這種特等病房還有會客室和辦公室，辦公室裡有完善的通訊設備，電話、傳真機、電腦、網路等等一應俱全。當初我們設計了這種病房，專門給那些大亨病人用的。大亨病人當然要有隱私權，所以特等病房有一個入口，而且二十四小時都有警衛看守，閒人勿進。

　　陳董事長患的是癌症，而且是末期，他很冷靜，知道大勢已去，只求不要太痛苦即可。當然像他這種人，

---

communication（n.）通訊　　　　　internet access（n.）上網
facility（n.）設備、工具

Chairman Chen stayed in a very particular part of our hospital, in what we might call the VIP suite, which actually included several rooms. In addition to a bed-room, this special medical suite included a meeting room, and an office with state-of-the-art communication facilities. There were telephones, a fax machine, a com-puter with Internet access, anything a special patient might require. From the beginning we only made the VIP medical suite available to patients of a particular economic status. Now, it stands to reason that patients of a particular economic status deserve special privacy rights. So the VIP suite had a private entrance and a security guard by the door twenty-four hours a day. There was no way in the world anyone could just walk in there out of the blue.

Chairman Chen was suffering from cancer, and it was in its last stages. He was usually very quiet. He

---

economic（n.）經濟上的、合算 deserve（v.）應得、應受
的、有利可圖的   privacy（n.）隱私、私生活

事業如此成功，叫他完全不管事，是不可能的，事業集團的極重要決定，他仍在管。可是他日漸消瘦，管的事情當然是越來越少了。

有一天他告訴我一件奇怪的事，他說他昨天晚上看到有人推了一輛手推車走過，車子上放滿了換洗的衣服及被單，好像要送去洗，推車的人非常瘦小，比他小很多，也比他瘦很多，而且跛腳，走起來一跛一跛的。就這麼巧，車子在他房門口翻倒了，那位瘦小又殘障的工友無法將車子扶起來，他站在門口，向他看著，一臉求

---

inevitably（adv.）不可避免地、必然地
incredibly（adv.）極為、難以置信地

administer（v.）掌管、經營
cart（n.）手推車、小車

knew what would inevitably happen. He asked only that it be as painless as possible. As was natural for a man of his stature, someone who had been so incredibly successful, to ask him to drop all contact with the business of his company was impossible. Actually, he was still making the most important policy decisions right up until the end. But day by day, he became thinner and thinner, and the affairs he administered eventually became fewer and fewer.

One day he told me of a strange event. He said that the night before, he had seen a man go by his room, pushing a hand cart. The cart was full of clothing and sheets, and it seemed the man was delivering them to the laundry department. The man pushing the cart was extremely thin, much smaller than Mr. Chen, and on top of that, he was crippled. One by one, every step he took was difficult. What a coincidence! The cart tumbled over

---

sheet（n.）床單
laundry（n.）洗衣店、洗衣房

crippled（adj.）跛腿的、殘廢的
coincidence（n.）巧合、巧事

助的表情，雖然沒有說話，董事長懂得他的意思。他在問：

「你願意幫我的忙嗎？」

我問陳董事長怎麼回答的，他說，他當時的回答是「我願意」。

我知道陳董事長是待病之身，何來力氣去將倒下的車子扶正？他說他事後也很奇怪他哪來的力量，可是他的確將車子扶正了，而且他發現那位工友推車的時候非常吃力，所以他就將車子推到了走廊的盡頭。

tiny（adj.）極小的、微小的　　　grasp（v.）領會、理解
pleading（adj.）懇求的

right in the doorway of his room. This tiny and physical-ly challenged worker didn't stand a chance getting that cart back upright again. He simply stood in the doorway of the suite and looked at Chairman Chen with a plead-ing expression on his face. Although he did not say a word, Mr. Chen grasped his meaning. The man was vir-tually asking, "Do you want to help me?"

I asked Chairman Chen how he replied, and he said his answer at that moment was "I want to."

Chairman Chen's health was extremely precarious. I knew that for a fact. How could he ever find the strength to set that cart upright? He said afterwards it seemed strange to him too, how he was strong enough, but he was actually able to do it. Indeed, since he

---

virtually（adv.）實際上、事實上　　precarious（adj.）不穩的、危險的

　　我知道這位董事長不會假造一個故事來騙我，他騙我幹嘛？可是，我覺得這件事情有點奇怪，我們醫院裡大概不會用殘障的人做這種推車的工作的，多危險？萬一出事，我們一定要吃上官司的，但是我並沒有將這件事情放在心上，我甚至想，也許陳先生病得很重了，有些幻想。

　　大概二個星期以後，陳先生又提起了那位殘障而瘦小的工友，他說這位工友常在晚上出現，他也一定會去

---

corridor（n.）走廊、迴廊
weird（adj.）怪誕的

challenged（adj.）殘障的
amuck（adv.）狂暴的、失控的

noticed how hard it had been for the worker to push the cart, Mr. Chen pushed it all the way to the end of the corridor for him.

Now, I fully knew this chairman of a great company could not possibly have cooked up a silly story to make a fool of me. What would be the point of lying to me? But I thought this entire affair was certainly weird. Our hospital would probably never have had a physically challenged person do this type of work. Pushing a cart? It was far too dangerous. Why, if anything ran amuck, the law would jump all over us in court. At the time, I didn't want to pay the matter any more mind. I simply figured that Mr. Chen was a very ill man, and his mind was playing tricks on him.

About two or so weeks passed by and then, again, Mr. Chen brought up this worker, so thin, so handicapped. He told me the worker had appeared again dur-

handicapped（adj.）有生理缺陷的、殘障的

幫他推車。這一次，我緊張起來了，因為這一定是不可能的事。我自己去問警衛，他們說從未有人在深夜進去過，也從未看到過殘障的工友。我去問了院方的總務處，他們說醫院裡不可能用殘障的工友做推車的工作，的確有人會去特等病房拿換洗的衣服，他們都是白天去的，晚上病人要睡覺休息，他們怎麼會去收衣服？

　　我將陳董事長的故事報告了院長，他認為這一定是陳先生的幻想，這個人是不可能存在的。

anxious（adj.）焦慮的　　　　　consult（v.）請教、磋商
resemble（v.）像、類似　　　　finance（n.）財務、金融

ing the night. He surely helped him push that cart again. This time, I really became anxious, because this entire situation was simply not possible. I had personally checked with the people in charge of security, and they assured me no one had managed to slip into the building there in the middle of the night. Neither had they seen anyone resembling the worker with a problem walking like that. I consulted the finance and personnel departments, who told me the hospital could not use a handicapped person for any job involving carts to push all over the place. It was the same with the question of retrieving laundry from the VIP suite section of the hospital. Workers did that during regular day shift hours. Patients needed their sleep at night. How could hospital staff possibly be banging around at that hour to pick up laundry?

I even told Chairman Chen's story to the director of the hospital. It was his estimation that the entire affair

---

retrieve（v.）收回、取回　　　　estimation（n.）評價、判斷

　　但是陳先生卻對這件事情很認真，我注意到他有一種很顯著的改變，在以前他對他的病感到相當地怨恨，總覺得不太能接受。可是最近，他的心思好像有些轉變了，有一天，他甚至約我好好地聊一聊。

　　他說他從來沒有看過如此不幸的人，他的孩子人人個子高大，體格都很好，他朋友的孩子們也都如此。他還是第一次看到一位如此瘦小的人，尤其令他感到不安的是，這個人還不良於行，是個殘障的人。

---

imagination（n.）幻想、妄想　　　　realm（n.）界、領域、範圍

had happened in Mr. Chen's imagination. It was beyond the realm of the possible for that worker to exist.

Chairman Chen, however, was absolutely earnest about it all.

I noticed that a change had come over him. He had previously appeared quite unhappy about his illness, and never seemed quite able to accept it. Recently, however, his attitude had turned a corner. One day he even went so far as to make an appointment with me to have a talk.

He said in the past he had never seen this type of unfortunate person. His own children were tall, and they enjoyed perfect health. The same was true of the children of his friends. This was the first time he ever saw someone so thin. What particularly bothered him was the fact that this man had trouble walking, was handicapped. Chairman Chen told me he had awakened early one

---

previously（adv.）事先、以前　　　bother（v.）使不安、使煩惱

　　陳董事長說他一天早晨醒來，忽然想通了，這種不幸的人一定早已存在的，只是他的世界中，沒有這種人，也許他曾經在街上看到過，但是他對這種人毫不關心，因此看到了，也等於沒有看到，這次他終於看到了。

　　陳先生是一個做事非常徹底的人，他的下屬在短期內替他在網路上找到了人類各種悲慘的照片和統計資料。他在電腦上將這些資料找出來給我看，他很感慨地

unfortunate（adj.）不幸、令人遺憾的　　　　gather（v.）聚集、收集

photograph（n.）照片

morning and the thought suddenly hit him that this type of unfortunate person surely had existed long ago. It was just that his world didn't have anyone like that. Perhaps he had seen people like this on the street, but he hardly ever cared about them. He had seen them, but been blind. This time he finally had eyes to see.

Mr. Chen was the type of person who, when he did anything, always did it all the way. In a short time, people working for him gathered photographs and related information on the Internet about a wide variety of people who were in all sorts of situations of suffering. He let me study this material he'd gleaned from Internet sources and, full of feeling, told me in all his 70 years of life, he had never imagined there were so many people suffering in the world.

---

related（adj.）有關的、相關的　　　glean（v.）點滴蒐集

告訴我，他過了七十幾年的日子，從來沒有想到世界上
有很多可憐的人。

　　我後來才知道陳先生的下屬都是極為能幹的人，只
要他說一句話，他們工作的結果都是非常好的，這些照
片往往都出自名家之手。網站上是找不到的，他們在全
世界的分公司前些日子都在找這些照片，大家都不懂為
什麼大老闆要找這些資料。

　　有一天，陳先生說以後大概不會再見到那位可憐的
工友了。這麼多的日子，這位工友沒有說過一句話，可
是那天晚上，當他又將車子推到走廊盡頭時，這位工友

---

baffle（v.）困惑　　　　　　　　pitiful（adj.）可憐的、令人同情的

Later I discovered that the members of his staff working at his command were supremely capable people. If he gave the word that such and such was to be done, you could bank on it: They took care of it, and produced amazing results. The photographs he had collected were taken by expert photographers and were not available on the Internet. Members from international branch offices had all been searching for such photos these days. Everyone was baffled why The Big Boss wanted all this material.

One day, Mr. Chen said from that time on, he probably would not see the pitiful worker any longer. After so many days, the worker had not said a word, but on that night, when he pushed the laundry cart to the end

向陳先生說：「你可以平安地回去了。」

　　我問陳董事長那位工友有沒有謝謝他，他反過來說是他應該謝謝這位工友。他過去生活得太好，所接觸的人沒有一個窮人，也沒有一個十分不幸而可憐的。

　　這次，他總算親眼看到了這種人，使他大開眼界。

　　事已至此，我覺得我必須講實話，我告訴陳董事長醫院裡沒有這樣的殘障工友，也沒有警衛看見他進來。陳董事長對這些話似乎不覺得有任何意義，他只說：「只要他要來，警衛是擋不住他的。」

hallway（n.）走廊、門廳　　　　nonplussed（adj.）迷惑的

of the hallway, he said to Mr. Chen, "You may go now in peace."

I asked Chairman Chen if the worker had said any word of thanks to him. He turned my words around and said it was he who should thank the worker. His previous life had been so good. He had never had contact with poor people, nor really with anyone who truly suffered.

For once in his life-this time-he had personally seen such a person. It had opened his eyes.

So the situation came to that point. I felt I had to set the facts straight. I told Chairman Chen that the hospital did not have any handicapped worker, and that the security team had never seen him entering the hospital. Chairman Chen was nonplussed by my words. His comment was, "If he really wanted to come, security could never stop him."

　　過了兩天，我被邀在陳董事長的遺囑上簽字作為證人，他在遺囑上指定了一家律師事務所負責，將他百分之九十的財產在十年內全部變賣成現金，然後將現金捐給窮人，雖然他的遺囑很短，卻有中英文對照，這家律師事務所也是以熟悉國際律法而著名的，至於捐給誰，他只指明由律師事務所找一批國內外的社會公正人士組成一個委員會來決定。

　　陳董事長在簽下遺囑以後，和大家一一握手，他很虛弱，沒有多說話，但他和我握手的時候，卻說：「你知道，我可以平安地回去了。」

participate（v.）參與
attorney（n.）律師、法定代理人
versed（adj.）熟練的、精通的

intricacies（n.）錯綜複雜的事務、紛繁難懂之處

Two days later, I was invited to participate as a witness in the signing of Chairman Chen's will. He had directed a lawyer from a firm to handle the responsibilities. He wanted 90% of his property to be converted to cash reserves in ten years. The cash was then to be freely distributed to poor people. Although his will was quite brief, it was printed bilingually, with Chinese on one side of the page, and English on the other. The attorney was well versed in the intricacies of international law. The specific beneficiaries of the donations, he required, were to be determined by a committee, formed by some local and international celebrities of sterling reputation at the invitation of the law firm.

After Chairman Chen signed the will, he shook hands with everyone present, one by one. His health looked very frail, and he didn't have much to say. When he shook hands with me, however, he said, "You know,

---

donation (n.) 捐獻、捐贈　　　　reputation (n.) 名譽、聲望
sterling (adj.) 優秀的　　　　　will (n.) 遺囑

　　當天，陳董事長在家人陪伴之下，平安地離開人世。

　　我將這件事的經過一五一十地告訴了陳董事長的兒子，他說他了解了這幾句話的意義了。他說他的爸爸一輩子都被社會上認為是一個極為能幹的人，其實他也有一顆柔軟的心，他也極有慈悲心，只是沒有被激發出來，沒有想到的是，在他臨終以前，有這麼一個遭遇，使他在臨終之時，完全換了一個人。

　　我決定問陳先生兒子一個很難回答的問題，我問他，「你認為真有那麼一位殘障工友嗎？」沒有想到他毫不猶豫地就回答「他絕對存在，只要你關懷這種人，

---

accomplished（adj.）有才華、能幹的　　encounter（n.）遭遇

I can go peacefully now."

That same day, in the company of his family, Chairman Chen left this world in peace.

After I told my story in great detail to Mr. Chen's son, he told me he now understood what the words meant. He said all through his life, his father had been considered a highly accomplished person in the eyes of society. In addition, however, he also had a great soft spot in his heart, a well of compassion inside of him. He just never had the opportunity to let it come out. He had never imagined that before he breathed his last, such an encounter would come along his path so that at the very end, he could change into another person.

I decided to ask Mr. Chen's son a question that was hard to answer. My question was, "Do you think that handicapped worker ever existed?" I was startled by his reply, which came without a second's hesitation.

---

hesitation（n.）猶豫、躊躇

你就會看到他。」

　　陳董事長的事情已經結束了，對我而言，我已不會再去追究究竟有沒有那位工友，我只希望能看到這種人。

　　　　　——原載二○○四年五月十三日《聯合報·副刊》

curious（adj.）稀奇古怪、好奇的

"He absolutely existed, sure he did. Only when you care about people like that can you see them."

Chairman Chen's curious affair has come to an end. As for me, I am finished with chasing after an answer about that worker. My only hope is that I too may have the eyes to see that person.

下　輯

李伯伯的英語課

英文糟，
大學教授也救不了

　　如果我是教育部長，我不會在乎一所學校有多少英文好的學生，而會在乎一所學校有多少英文奇差的學生。好的教育家，永遠是要將最低程度拉起來的，只會教好天才的人，根本不配被稱為是教育家。

教育部長杜正勝對大學生英文程度作了一種願望性的宣示，他希望在民國九十六年，百分之五十的大學生會通過全民英檢的中級程度；同年，百分之五十的技術學院學生可以通過全民英檢的初級程度，我雖然歡迎杜部長對於英語能力的重視，我仍然希望部長從另一個角度來看這個問題。

首先，我認為大學生（包含技術學院的學生），如果英文程度非常不好，大學教授是無技可施的。因為大學教授的專長，並不是教普通的英文。

大學生英文有多差？我建議政府做一個簡單的測驗，請同學們翻譯一些簡單的中文句子，或將一些不太難的文章翻譯成中文，我敢擔保，只有極少數的同學可以在中翻英時，不犯文法上的基本錯誤。至於閱讀的能力，不要說看《紐約時報》了，就看國內英文報紙，絕大多數的學生都有困難。我們理工科教授最近發現很多大學生，根本無法看英文的教科書，更無法看英文的學術論文。有一位明星大學的畢業生，居然不認識university，同一學校的畢業生，不會念engineering。

問題不在大學教育，在於國中和高中，部長應該知道有四分之一的國中畢業生，基本學力測驗的分數不到八十八分。試問，這些同學的英文程度夠好嗎？這些學生一定有高中、高職可念，他們也都可能進入大學或技術學院，在這種情況之下，大學以及技術學院之中，當然會有很多英文程度不好的同學。

我們討論大學生的英文程度，而一字不提國中生的英文程度，大概是將注意力集中到那些英文程度還不太差的同學那裡去，至於程度太差的，教育部好像要放棄他們。我知道這是必然的結果，整個國家就是只注意菁英教育。教改就是由菁英份子替菁英份子設計出來的。

我更希望教育部知道，教育部一旦宣示了對英文的重視，各級學校校長們的反應，一定是宣佈一些華而不實的政策，某某大學會說學生一定要通過某某英文檢定，才能畢業；但是他們心知肚明，他們大多數的學生是不可能通過這種檢定考試的，因此他們在辦法上留有但書，也就是這種學生必須選修某種高階英文課，校長們都知道，這種課，絕大多數的學生都會及格的，所以這種政策之下，最後人人仍然都畢業了，好者恆好，壞者恆壞。

技術學院的校長們也會忽然將英文課本變得很難。他們認為將來萬一有人來參觀，一看到如此難的英文課本，立刻佩服得五體投地，至於學生懂不懂呢？他們也管不了。我常碰到一些技術學院的老師們向我抱怨英文課本太難，根本忽視學生程度差的事實，學生們學不會，老師們有無力感，但是至少這所學校給了外界一個重視英文的印象。

當務之急乃是在於各校發展出一種「務實」的英文教學辦法，即注意學生的程度。前些日子，我注意到在信義鄉的一所小學，那裡的校長選了一批英文句子，每一週學生都要背一些英文句子，這些句子每週會公佈出來，如此一年，這些孩子至少在畢業之前，能夠背出相當多的生字，也能背很多的英文句子，這種做法，就是我所謂的務實做法：注意學生的程度，打好學生的基礎。

如果我是教育部長，我不會在乎一所學校有多少英文好的學生，而會在乎一所學校有多少英文奇差的學生。好的教育家，永遠是要將最低程度拉起來的，只會教好天才的人，根本不配被稱為是教育家。目前，很多學校，雖然有大批同學程度奇差，校長也不在乎，因為他只要有少數頂尖的畢業生能考上明星學校，他就可以向社會大眾交差。

所以，也許在三年以後，的確有更多的學生英文進步了，但是由於校方傾全力教那些有潛力的學生，那些英文程度不好的學生可能程度更加低落了。

我還是要老調重談，頂尖學生的英文程度不夠好，也許值得我們重視；但是英文的最低程度，才是一切問題之所在，也是我們最該注意的事，他們將來不要談是否有國際觀，因為英文差，一路都跟不上，變成了毫無競爭力的一群，收入一定會低。他們的潛力也永遠不能發揮，永遠是弱勢，這才是教育部長該注意的事。也許部長應該定出一個願景，將我們學生的英文最低程度，能夠逐年的提高。

——原載二○○四年九月九日《聯合報》

考試出難題，
羞辱學生菜英文

　　我在此拜託全國的老師們，不要放棄英文不好的學生，儘量給他們鼓勵，儘量教得容易一點，儘量反覆練習，平時一再地叫他們做簡單的造句，有了錯，立刻就改過來，他們將來就不會再犯錯了。

昨天晚報報導很多英文界學者談到大學生英文程度低落，這實在不該算是新聞了。研究生中都有人會說「I is」，「I has」等等奇怪的句子。每一年都會有研討會來檢討英文教學，每一次都講同樣的話，每一年的大學生英文都是原地踏步走，為什麼？我認為這是因為很多教英文的老師們不肯面對現實的緣故。

大學生英文不好，當然不能怪大學教授，甚至不能怪高中老師，我們必須很坦白地承認，這些英文程度不好的大學生，他們在國中時，英文就沒有學好，但是，我們現在在小學，就已經開始教英文了，因此，我們必須先檢討小學的英文教育。

我國的小學生，每週只有兩小時的英文課，也不是全部老師都會教英文，有些偏遠地區，至今沒有足夠的合格英文老師，常要靠替代役或者代課老師來教英文，小學生學不好英文，乃是意料中的事。為什麼那些偏遠地區的小學沒有英文老師呢？因為名額不夠了。很多偏遠地區的小學生越來越少，教育部無法再給那些小學新的名額，本來就沒有英文老師的學校，就只好一直沒有英文老師了。

如果完全靠學校，小學生很難將英文學好，但是很多家境好的小學生可以進補習班，或者請家教，因此英文好得不得了。這種現象，在小學裡，沒有什麼關係，可是一到了國中，情形就非常不妙了。

很多國中老師，面臨很多家長的壓力，認為英文應該越難越好，弱勢孩子的家長多半沒有任何聲音，他們絕對不會要求老師教得容易一點，考得容易一點。其結果是國中老師的英文考題，往往是弱勢團體孩子絕對無法招架的。

舉例來說，有人打電話給我，說他孩子幾乎要完全放棄英文，我終於看到了他小孩的英文考卷，這是國中一年級第一次月考的考卷，短短的四行字裡有以下的生字：report, hunting, special, honest, clean, right, gentle, giant, afraid, social, gun, wonder, people, animal, information，這位國中生是鄉下孩子，他的父母完全不懂英文，所住的地方沒有補習班，即使有補習班，他的父母也無力送他去。

這種專門替程度好學生設計的英文教育，使很多國中生上英文課就是發呆的時候。可是我們的教育制度是沒有品質管制的，他們可以從國中畢業，也可以進入高中，當然也變成了大學生，難怪有英文老師發現，有些研究生用了「I is」，我本人就看過「I has」，當時實在嚇了一跳。

如果教育部官員真的想提升大學生的英文程度，就必須從小學做起。英文說容易不容易，說難也不難，如果小學老師肯將英文課變成一種反覆練習的課，再笨的小孩子也會說「I am」，而不是「I is」了。

品質管制仍然是重要的，我們一定要知道小孩子的英文程度有無進步。我不是小學英文老師，但我在埔里負責一個博幼基金會，專門幫助弱勢小孩子，我們有一套控管的機制，因此我們知道每一位小孩子的英文到了什麼程度，很多當年英文一個字都不會的孩子，在這種反覆練習，又有品質管制的教法之下，他們可以順利地進入國中，我最近看了一份報告，發現好多同學第一次月考全班第一名。

我在此拜託全國的老師們，不要放棄英文不好的學生，盡量給他們鼓勵，盡量教得容易一點，盡量反覆練習，平時一再地叫他們做簡單的造句，有了錯，立刻就改過來，他們將來就不會再犯錯了。

我的學生，拿到了碩士學位，已經在大公司做事，依然每週要做中翻英，我也一定替他們改。一開始的時候，他們幾乎個個錯誤百出，可是每週被我改一次，就不會犯嚴重錯誤了。

如果老師們平時不管學生究竟學會了什麼，一到考試，就用難題來羞辱學生。每一年，那些大學教授們會發現，又有大學生在寫「I has」，「He have」等等的句子了。

——原載二○○五年十一月十四日《聯合報》

一個句子兩個動詞，
英文教育犯了「最基本的錯」

　　我們的英文教育並不注重基本的文法。大多數老師注意的是文法裡的較難部分，至於文法中最基本的部分，絕對不會出現在考題之中。英文教育一定要務實，也就是說應該要明訂共同的目標：學生寫英文句子不犯基本文法錯誤。

在中文裡，兩個動詞，當然是可以同時出現在句子裡，「我喜歡念書」、「我不愛聽音樂」這些都是正確無誤的句子。可是在英文裡，兩個動詞連在一起用，卻是犯了大忌。

因此，這次教育部的官員們，寫出了「Each party is reasonably provide access to research」，就引起了軒然大波，因為「is」和「provide」都是動詞。這種錯誤，我稱之為「致命的錯誤」，我的學生如果犯了這種錯誤，我會寫上FE，意思是你犯了一個fatal error。

雖然媒體對這件事大肆炒作，我可一點都不以為奇，因為我相信，絕大多數學生會犯這種錯誤。我在大學裡教了好多年的英文，我也每週都參加研究生論文研討會，我深知同學的英文程度，容我說一句不中聽的話，他們就是一群會犯基本文法錯誤的人。

我不喜歡在此嘲笑任何人，我們應該深刻地檢討，為什麼學生會犯這種最基本的文法錯誤？我們的學生，國中時就念了三年英文，在高中，又念了三年英文；進高中，要考英文，進大學，又要考英文，但是為什麼不會基本的文法呢？

道理非常簡單，我們的英文教育並不注重基本的文法。大多數老師注意的是文法裡的較難部分，虛擬語氣、冠詞等等都是老師們的最愛，至於文法中最基本的部分，絕對不會出現在考題之中。

一直到現在，大學生常忘了在動詞後面加s，忘了有時一定要用has，而不能用have。他們也會在must或can的後面加上to，在使用現在完成式的時候，又忘了用過去分詞，至於兩個動詞連在一起用，更是家常便飯。

儘管這些同學如此糊塗，只要給他們當頭棒喝，幾次以後，他們就不會犯基本文法錯誤了。我的學生每週要寫一篇短短的中翻英，暨大有一個改英文作文的電腦系統，每次我改作文，一定一面口呼學生的名字，一面解釋他錯在那裡，當然也警告他以後不得再犯，這些動作，全部由電腦記錄下來，事後學生可以看到，也可聽到我告誡他的聲音。一年下來，大概不會再犯這種基本而致命的錯誤了。

我每個週末都要改一百篇左右的文章，每一個錯誤，都列入檔案，下一次上課時會向同學們解釋這些錯誤應該如何改正。每週改一百篇英文作文，不是一件令人心情愉快的事。每次改作文以前，一定要吃降血壓的藥，以防看到荒謬的文章，會一命嗚呼也。但是到了學期結束時，眼見同學們犯錯的機會越來越小，血壓藥大概就不再需要了。

　　我要在此向社會提出嚴重警告，全國的英文考試都沒有注意到英文的最基本部分。即使學生通過了考試，仍不能請他寫英文文章。我就握有證據，我有學生寫英文作文時，錯誤百出，但是他卻在國家舉辦的重要考試中，考到了高分。

　　英文教育一定要務實，也就是說應該要明訂共同的目標：學生寫英文句子不犯基本文法錯誤。有些時候，學生上的課，看起來內容偉大無比，但是學生的基本功力其實不行。老師們總對將學生打好基礎的工作沒有興趣，只想教那些極有學問的東西，考也是考那些有學問的東西。學生好像已經學到了極高深的學問，其實，一旦叫他寫文章，他就會很起勁地將兩個動詞連在一起用。

　　有一次，一名同學一口氣用了三個動詞，他說他只知道不可以用兩個動詞，所以他用三個動詞，這下大概是正確的了。

　　如果我們的英文考試仍然奇難無比，而絲毫不理會學生會不會犯基本文法的錯誤，我只有勸政府官員們不要叫部下寫什麼英文文件，以免丟人現眼也。

　　學生可以不犯基本文法錯誤的，如果他們從小就不做選擇題，而是真槍實彈地寫英文句子和英文作文，一旦犯了錯，老師會告訴他。政府官員就不要再害怕部下寫出了奇怪的英文文章。

——原載二○○四年十月二十三日《聯合報》民意論壇

不知道「I」是什麼，
也不知道「am」是什麼

　　如果一位老師在教一位大人物的孩子，他一定會非常認真，因為他多多少少有點怕那一位大人物家長來興師問罪，弱勢家庭的家長是不會來興師問罪的，他們常以為自己笨，自己的孩子也笨。

基本學力測驗才考完，社會的焦點全部都在哪一位同學考到最高分，或者進入建中、一女中要二百九十分，而大家忽略了我們同一國家內就有大批的同學考得一塌糊塗。

有考得不好的學生，乃是正常的現象，但是如果偏遠地區的孩子們幾乎都考得不好，以及考得不好的同學幾乎都在偏遠地區，這就值得我們注意了。不幸的是，我們要面臨一個殘酷的事實：就教育而言，我們有很大的城鄉差距。在偏遠的鄉下，有很多國中生的基本學力測驗平均分數只有六十分，有一所就在新竹市附近的一所鄉下國中，學力測驗最高分只是一○八分。這種情形也使偏遠地區高中老師痛苦不堪，因為他們所收的學生基測成績只有一百分左右。

有一位高工電機科老師告訴我，他的學生幾乎全部不會分數加減，有些同學連英文二十六個字母都寫不完全。國中生基測成績落後，不能責怪國中老師，因為有很多國中生入學的時候就已經根基不好，國中老師無論如何努力，都已無法使他們跟上進度。我們可以說國中生基測成績不理想，完全是因為我們的小學品質管制的緣故。

我有一次發現一批孩子在做減法習題，他們是五年級的小學生，我又發現曾經有很多小四學生不會加法，至於英文，那就更嚴重了。好多小學畢業的孩子英文字一個也不認識。

我們如果真的要幫助基測不好的孩子，一定要在小學教育上下手，小學教育的品質管制並不是要孩子留級，而是一定要使學生至少通過最低的門檻，整數的加減乘除，小數點的加減乘除，甚至分數的加減乘除，都是絕大多數孩子一定可以學會的，如果老師知道某某同學連最基本的學問都沒有，就必須以因材施教的方式去幫助他，他一定學得會的。

現在有很多課輔機構，專門幫助功課不好的孩子，他們大概都不能將一個偏遠地區的孩子程度大幅提高，但是他們都能將孩子的程度提高到跨越了最低門檻，可見孩子們的程度提高到某一地位，是有希望的。

如何使學生不至於太落後呢？我認為教育部必須讓偏遠地區的小學能多聘老師，有了足夠的老師，老師們就可以要求孩子做完功課再回家。目前偏遠地區的孩子們大多數家庭都比較貧困，父母很多都不在家，即使在家，也不會督促孩子做家庭作業，有些孩子在家裡連書桌都沒有。如果孩子們每天再多留兩小時，將該做的練習都做完，他們不可能會全跟不上進度的。

如果無法多聘老師，也應該以補助方式，使老師們肯在課餘督促孩子做家庭作業，孩子如果有問題，也可以當天就問老師。重點是：教育部一定要知道老師輔導以後，學生的程度有沒有進步。

目前，偏遠地區小學的另一個嚴重問題是英文老師的缺乏，很多鄉的全部小學中。沒有一位合格的正式老師，必須靠代課老師或者替代役老師，很多小學生一週只上兩小時英文課，這種情形他們如何能在國中畢業後考到好的基測成績。

教育部一定要籌到經費，讓偏遠地區的小學能多聘合格而正式的英文老師。需知很多城裡的小學生在小學四年級就已會用英文做作文。而我們鄉下的一些孩子卻在完全無人管的狀況下進入了國中。我最近發現一位國中一年級下學期的學生，不知道I是什麼，當然也不知道am是什麼了。

如果一位老師在教一位大人物的孩子，他一定會非常認真，因為他多多少少有點怕那一位大人物家長來興師問罪，弱勢家庭的家長是不會來興師問罪的，他們常以為自己笨，自己的孩子也笨。我希望教育部的官員能扮演弱勢家庭家長的角色，代他們發言，代他們關心弱勢孩子的學習進度。我敢打賭，教育上的城鄉差距會大幅度減小的。

——原載二○○七年六月十八日《中國時報》

救語文能力，
大量閱讀是妙方

閱讀不夠的孩子，也有詞不達意的痛苦，即使他已看懂了某篇論文，他也無法將它的大意濃縮成幾句話，不要說生動了，就連正確無誤都不一定能辦到，遑論描繪自己的想法。

這次很多人發起重視國語文教育的運動，並受到了國人的重視。

語文能力不好，會影響學習任何學門的能力。我就教過一個小學生，每次看到一個文字敘述很長的題目就會慌，而且第一個反應就是「我不會」，一旦將題意解釋給他聽，他立刻就將題目做出來了。

我還聽過一個故事，有一位數學老師覺得他的學生老是不會做數學題目，他請了一位國文老師來解釋題意，學生就會做了。我也碰到一位化學老師，她的經驗相同，大多數弱勢同學之所以不會做題目，都是因為看不懂題意。

國語文能力差，絕不是寫別字而已，最嚴重的就是看不懂文章。不相信的話，可以找一位程度差的同學讀福爾摩斯探案，他很可能弄不清楚人物互相錯綜複雜的關係，更弄不清破案的關鍵。亞森羅蘋就好得多了，大概是因為其中邏輯推理的成份不多的緣故，至於克莉絲蒂的偵探小說，那是最高境界，能徹底看懂兇莉絲蒂小說的小孩子，已經不算是弱勢孩子了。

閱讀不夠的孩子，也有詞不達意的痛苦，即使他已看懂了某篇論文，他也無法將它的大意濃縮成幾句話，不要說生動了，就連正確無誤都不一定能辦到，遑論描繪自己的想法。更嚴重的是：很多文章不是詞不達意，而是前後文互相矛盾。你問他為何會寫出如此互相矛盾的文章，他也只有苦笑並不知道原因。

很多人以為只有學文法科的人需要有好的語文能力，其實學理工的同學一樣需要語文能力。做研究要寫論文，如果語文能力不好，寫出來的論文沒有人能看得懂，即使看懂了，也可能給人一種內容貧乏的印象。大多數工程師不要寫論文，但是要做報告，情形亦是如此。很多工程師做事的能力雖然很強，但是不會向上司解釋成果，吃很大的虧。

閱讀不多的弱勢同學，知識當然不多，寫文章時不可能引經據典，而且因為所知者少，寫出來的文章當然了無新意，談話的時候也不可能有趣。

我希望我們的年輕人有以下的語文能力：

一、可以很快地看懂文章，而且抓到文章的重點。
二、可以正確、清楚地表達自己的想法。
三、表達想法時合乎邏輯，不會自相矛盾。
四、表達的想法不落俗套，有獨到的見解。

要得到這種能力，其實不難，只要大量閱讀即可。我在此建議給弱勢孩子閱讀的書籍文章：

經典名著

任何書籍或文章，已經成為永垂不朽者，一定有其道理，唸了絕對有益。古文當然屬於此類，外國的著名小說，也很該念。最近英國政府在英國監獄強迫受刑人唸英國著名小說，結果好多受刑人出獄後，努力進入大學專攻英國文學。據統計，最受受刑人歡迎的小說是《蒼蠅王》。

好的論述文章

比方說，重要報紙的社論和讀者投書。我並非說這種文章有真理存在，而是因為這些文章條理必定很清楚，中心思想也很明確，絕不會天馬行空，更不是老生常譚。而且這些文章常常有知識性，比方說，有一篇社論也許會談到預算，孩子會從此知道國家是有預算制度的。當然，選擇這些文章時必須避免有太多政治性的。

法官判決文和偵探小說

兩者的共同特點就是講究邏輯。很少人會發現法官的判決文有互相矛盾的地方，好的偵探小說更是如此。英國的

《泰晤士報》有專門的法律版，常有法官的判決文，可惜我國不太重視這些。很多法官的判決文硬邦邦，很難讀，不過，我曾經看過一些大法官的判決文，的確精采無比，其思慮不但清晰，而且任何可能的疑問，都會在判決文中提到，令人心服口服。偵探小說的優點則是有創意。要寫出有趣而又天衣無縫的偵探小說，是要有很深功力的。

有趣味的知識性文章

在此，我建議大家看《人間福報》的一些有趣報導，大多數的文章是有關科學的，一概很短，非常適合孩子們看。看了以後，可以增加知識。

其實，菁英份子的孩子們，國文程度並不差，弱勢團體的孩子，才是問題之所在。教育部決定恢復在考高中學力測驗加考作文，沒有人反對，但我卻大為憂心，對於弱勢孩子而言，這個措施是雪上加霜，和城裡孩子相比，他們不太可能寫得出好的作文來，原因很簡單，他們通常沒有看什麼課外書，對於很多事情，根本沒有什麼觀念，如何寫得出好的作文來？

我在埔里的博幼基金會就強迫孩子們大量閱讀，很多小孩子會在同學間有意無意中談到他們讀課外書所得到的知識，使同學們對他們另眼相看。有些已經迷上了金庸的小說，迷上福爾摩斯的孩子也不少。我在想募款購置克莉絲蒂的全套，看看這些弱勢孩子會不會迷上這位大作家的名著。

我承認我的想法屬於異類，因為我自己屬於什麼書都看的人，因此我把我的經驗介紹給各位，各位老師和家長，不妨參考也。

——原載二〇〇五年一月十五日《聯合報》民意論壇

譯者簡介

康士林（Daniel J. Bauer）

美國威斯康辛大學比較文學博士。天主教神父，現為輔仁大學英國語文學系副教授兼進修部英文系主任。近年來，英譯的中文短篇故事，散見於 *The Chinese Pen*、*The Free China Review* 及 *Inter-religio*（香港）等期刊。自一九九五年九月以來，即每星期為英文《中國郵報》（*The Chinese Pen*）撰寫專欄，討論有關教育及社會議題。目前在輔仁大學英國語文學系所開設的課程有翻譯、十八世紀英國文學、二十世紀初美國文學等。

康士林（Nicholas Koss）

美國印第安那大學比較文學博士，現任輔仁大學比較文學研究所所長。自一九八一年起於輔仁大學英國語文學系任教迄今。康教授並於輔仁大學比較文學研究所與翻譯學研究所授課。最近剛卸下六年任期的外語學院院長行政職。康教授著作有：專書 *The Best and Fairest Land: Medieval Images of China*（台北 1999），數篇比較文學相關學術論文及台灣 *The Chinese Pen* 翻譯文章。

校訂者簡介

強勇傑

國立台灣大學外國語文學系所畢業,現為國立台灣師範大學翻譯研究所博士生。擔任中華民國筆會中英核對多年。八十九年獲第十三屆梁實秋文學獎短篇小說中譯英優選,九十年獲第一屆文建會文學翻譯獎譯詩組中譯英佳作,九十一年獲第十五屆梁實秋文學獎譯文組英譯中優等獎;九十二年獲第二屆文建會文學翻譯獎譯文組中譯英佳作。

繪者簡介

官月淑

嘉義人,國立藝專畢業,現為家庭主婦。喜歡閱讀和美食,習慣用紙、筆紀錄生活週遭,享受與兒子一起散步的時光。

版權所有　翻印必究

九歌譯叢 933

跟李伯伯學英文1：Page 21（有聲書）

著　　　者：李 家 同

譯　　　者：康 士 林、鮑 端 磊

校　　　訂：強 勇 傑

繪　　　者：官 月 淑

責 任 編 輯：何 靜 婷

發 行 人：蔡 文 甫

發 行 所：九歌出版社有限公司

　　　　　臺北市八德路3段12巷57弄40號

　　　　　電話／02-25776564・傳眞／02-25789205

　　　　　郵政劃撥／0112295-1

九歌文學網：www.chiuko.com.tw

登 記 證：行政院新聞局局版臺業字第1738號

印 刷 所：晨捷印製股份有限公司

法 律 顧 問：龍躍天律師・蕭雄淋律師・董安丹律師

朗 讀 版：2009（民國98）年08月10日

定　　價：280元

ISBN 978-957-444-613-1　　　　　Printed in Taiwan

書號：f0933

（缺頁、破損或裝訂錯誤，請寄回本公司更換）

國家圖書館出版品預行編目資料

跟李伯伯學英文1：Page21（有聲書）／李家同著；
康士林,鮑端磊譯. ── 初版. ──臺北市：
九歌, 民98.08
　　面： 公分. ──（九歌譯叢；933）
朗讀版
中英對照
ISBN　978-957-444-613-1　　　（平裝）

1.英語　2.讀本

805.18　　　　　　　　　　　　　　98011658